MR BOWLING BUYS A NEWSPAPER

'THE DETECTIVE STORY CLUB is a clearing house for the best detective and mystery stories chosen for you by a select committee of experts. Only the most ingenious crime stories will be published under the THE DETECTIVE STORY CLUB imprint. A special distinguishing stamp appears on the wrapper and title page of every THE DETECTIVE STORY CLUB book—the Man with the Gun. Always look for the Man with the Gun when buying a Crime book.'

Wm. Collins Sons & Co. Ltd., 1929

Now the Man with the Gun is back in this series of COLLINS CRIME CLUB reprints, and with him the chance to experience the classic books that influenced the Golden Age of crime fiction.

THE DETECTIVE STORY CLUB

FURTHER TITLES IN PREPARATION

MR BOWLING BUYS A NEWSPAPER

A STORY OF CRIME

BY

DONALD HENDERSON

WITH AN INTRODUCTION BY
MARTIN EDWARDS

COLLINS
CRIME
CLUB

COLLINS CRIME CLUB
An imprint of HarperCollins*Publishers*
1 London Bridge Street
London SE1 9GF
www.harpercollins.co.uk

This Detective Story Club edition 2018

First published in Great Britain by Constable & Co. 1943

Introduction © Martin Edwards 2018

A catalogue record for this book is available from the British Library

ISBN 978-0-00-826531-1

For more information visit: www.harpercollins.co.uk/green

INTRODUCTION

DONALD HENDERSON'S *Mr Bowling Buys a Newspaper* earned considerable acclaim when it was first published in 1943, but for many years the book has been out of print. This neglect seems unaccountable, given that its admirers included Raymond Chandler. As readers of this welcome reissue will find, Henderson crafted a distinctive work of fiction; what is more, the story behind it is equally intriguing, while the tale of the author's life is not only thought-provoking but also poignant.

Chandler wrote 'The Simple Art of Murder', his critical essay about the crime genre, which famously proclaims 'down these mean streets a man must go who is not himself mean, who is neither tarnished nor afraid', for the *Atlantic Monthly*. It appeared in December 1944, not long after Henderson's book was published. Having flayed several leading writers of classic whodunits, Chandler talked at length about Dashiell Hammett's gift for writing realistic crime fiction, before saying: 'Without him there might not have been . . . an ironic study as able as Raymond Postgate's *Verdict of Twelve* . . . or a tragi-comic idealization of the murderer as in Donald Henderson's *Mr Bowling Buys a Newspaper* . . .'

To have one's book name-checked by such a major author, and in an essay which has been much-quoted over the years, would be a fillip to any struggling novelist's career. Tragically, Henderson did not gain any long-term benefit from it; less than three years later he was dead, at the age of 41. In the course of his short and often troubled life, however, he published fourteen novels, as well as non-fiction books, stage plays and radio plays.

Until recently, little was known about Henderson, and even

less had been written about him and his work. Thanks to the diligent and invaluable research of Paul T. Harding, much information has come to light, and Henderson's fragmentary archive has been presented to the University of Reading. Paul Harding has also edited an unpublished memoir written by Henderson; its title *The Brink* comes from the final sentence, which sums up the author's bleak worldview: 'There is always a chasm gaping at one's feet, and although merry enough about it, most people finally get a little tired of hovering on the brink.'

Donald Landels Henderson was born in 1905; he had a twin sister, but their mother died four days after giving birth. Henderson's twin, Janet, also died in childbirth, when she was 28. Their father re-married when the twins were four, and Henderson was to say, 'I cannot pretend to have enjoyed anything very much about my childhood or adolescence.' He was educated at public school, and under pressure from his businessman father he took up a career in farming. But agricultural life didn't suit Henderson, and a stint as a publisher's salesman brought only misery. He enjoyed better fortune working for a stockbroker, but he abandoned the City in his mid-twenties during a turbulent period when he suffered a nervous breakdown.

Since his teens, he had enjoyed acting, and had also dreamed of becoming a writer. He joined a touring repertory company, and married an actress called Janet Morrison, a single parent who later gave up her son for adoption. The marriage soon failed, and the couple separated, although they did not divorce for some years.

Henderson began to combine writing with his acting career, but this was a period of worldwide economic depression—'the Slump'—and money was always short. Chapter titles in *The Brink* such as 'Poverty Street', 'Another Failure', 'Disaster', and 'The Awfulness of Everything' give unequivocal clues to his melancholy during much of the Thirties. He had parts in plays such as *Rope* by Patrick Hamilton, a writer with whose dark thrillers his own work is sometimes bracketed.

After a failed theatrical venture in London, 'I was not in a fussy mood . . . I got a room in Surbiton . . . and in a fearful burst of enthusiasm I sat down and wrote three novels running, scarcely leaving myself time to think them out, so anxious was I to get farther and farther away from the brink of the precipice.' The books in question were *Teddington Tragedy*, *His Lordship the Judge* and *Murderer at Large*, and they were published between October 1935 and October 1936. In his memoir, Henderson supplies little detail about the influences on his crime fiction, although he acknowledges that the nineteenth-century case of the serial killer William Palmer was an inspiration for *Murderer at Large*.

Henderson's account in his memoir of his time in farming gives, perhaps unintentionally, a hint about the dark side of his mind: 'There were a lot of rats on the farm and I enjoyed many a rat hunt with the dogs. Sometimes you didn't need dogs . . . We were constantly rat trapping, at which I became really expert, and I know of few greater thrills, including getting a book accepted, than hurrying along next morning to see if you have caught anything and finding that two angry, terrified little eyes are staring at you murderously. Or even more than two.' His account of the homicidal career of Erik Farmer (was the surname a nod to his previous profession?), the loathsome protagonist of *Murderer at Large*, is equally chilling.

Procession to Prison, a crime novel about a 'trunk murderer', appeared in 1937; it was well received, but thereafter Henderson 'could sell nothing I wrote for fully two years . . . The irony of the literary life, as I have experienced it, seems to lie in the fact that, when you are all but down and out, you can write well, but your luck is never any good from the *selling* point of view. Poverty breeds more poverty.' Henderson tramped the streets of London and Edinburgh looking for work 'with my press cutting book under my arm', but without success. He had lost his nerve as an actor, and seems—although the chronology of his memoir is vague—to have spent two summers camping out in the open. After a spell in hospital, he tried to put together a book of famous trials, but failed to interest a publisher in the project.

He had better luck with a comedy thriller play called *The Secret Mind*, but his attempts to enlist for military service were rebuffed, and he became an ambulance driver, only to be badly injured during the blitz in September 1940. The following year, deemed unfit even for work in civil defence, he started to write a new novel—*Mr Bowling Buys a Newspaper*.

Henderson's explanation in *The Brink* of the concept he had for the book was striking: 'It was to be a religious novel, but because publishers and everyone were always so terrified of religion, or bitter about it, unless very delicately presented, I would also make it a murder novel, to help the sales. It had a magnificent plot—though I am bad at plots—and of course I should be told I had written a "detective" story because there happened to be a detective in it. But that didn't matter, as long as I sold it. It would be, for a change, about a man who wanted to get caught, and hanged, because he was rather browned off about life in general . . . I broke my rule and started this book without knowing for certain what the end would be . . . I decided that there must be plenty of humour in the book, to take the edge off the sombre, brooding background . . . I wrote the book with fearful haste and enthusiasm . . . in about a week and a half, straight onto the typewriter.'

The book struggled at first to find a publisher, and after another spell of acting, Henderson joined the BBC. Finally, things began to look up. He again came across Rosemary ('Roses') Bridgwater, who had been his girlfriend many years earlier, and once he had secured a divorce from his first wife, they married and moved into a flat in Chelsea. The novel eventually sold both in Britain and the US, and attracted positive reviews. Not everyone, however, was as impressed as Raymond Chandler. In *The Brink*, Henderson quoted a letter sent to his publishers by someone from Edinburgh who signed themselves as 'Lover of Clean-Minded Literature' which began:

'I have read *Mr Bowling Buys a Newspaper* and paid 8/6d for it. With the exception of Mrs Agatha Christie and also Miss Anna Buchan, I will never again buy a book without first hearing it recommended by a friend. This book is the last word in filth and should never have been printed by you . . .'

For Henderson, though, the popularity of the book 'made up to me for years of despair'. He wrote a new crime novel, *Goodbye to Murder*, in about ten days, and adapted *Mr Bowling Buys a Newspaper* for the stage. His wife gave birth to a son in January 1945, although a second son, born in December of the same year, died when only a few days old. The play of the book was staged in 1946, achieving critical success, and the film rights were sold. At this point, the manuscript of *The Brink* comes to a rather abrupt end. Henderson's health was failing, and he died of lung cancer on 18 April 1947. Although *Mr Bowling Buys a Newspaper* was televised live by the BBC in 1950, and again in 1957, inevitably his reputation began to fade.

Yet his writing, at its best, is distinctive enough to deserve reconsideration. The principal influences on his crime fiction are surely not Hammett, as Chandler suggested, but rather C. S. Forester, author of *Payment Deferred* (Henderson's memoir mentions the homicidal protagonist, William Marble, in the context of a discussion about Charles Laughton, who played Marble in the stage and film versions of the book) and Francis Iles, author of *Malice Aforethought* and *Before the Fact*. Forester and Iles wrote with a chilly irony that also runs through Henderson's work, and that of other occasional crime novelists of the period, such as C. E. Vulliamy, Bruce Hamilton and Raymond Postgate. 'I would not like to say where my fascination for murder and disturbed mental conditions came from,'

Henderson said. Whatever its origins, it resulted in his producing a handful of books as unorthodox as they are powerful.

MARTIN EDWARDS
July 2017
www.martinedwardsbooks.com

With love
to Roses

NOTE

THE characters in this book are fictitious; no portrayal of any person, living or dead, is intended.

CHAPTER I

MR BOWLING sat at the piano until it grew darker and darker, not playing, but with Tchaikovsky's Piano Concerto in D Flat Minor opened before him at the first movement, rubbing his hands nervously, and staring across the shadowy room to the window, to see if it was dark enough yet. The window was wide open, and at first the evening was a kind of green, such as you would expect in a London summer, then it got grey, then it got muddy brown; then it turned black and safe. It was not that he was going to do anything very special, but he got into moods when he didn't care to talk to people. In just the same way, he often got into desperately lonely moods; moods which might have been called suicidal, had he not been a man incapable of committing suicide, for he had too much of a sense of humour for such a cold and deliberate act. He went quietly past the little telephone cupboard, paused outside his door and listened. Then he stole past the two doors and the thin staircase which led to the top floor, taking the broader staircase down to the second, and then the first floor. He passed various doors on the ground floor and slipped out into the square and was soon in Notting Hill Gate. In his public school accent, he asked for an *Evening Standard*. When there wasn't one left, he said he would take anything, he didn't care, on this occasion, what the paper was. It wasn't war news he was after, he had put the war out of his mind, so far as it was possible. He was bored with war and felt entitled to be. You could regard it as peace time if you liked, if you had a good imagination. He stumbled along in the blackout to the Coach and Horses, where it was cheery, and where one of the barmaids wasn't too bad, though seeing her made him decide once again: 'I'll never kill a woman again! Not on your life! Things happen you don't expect!' All the

same, he'd had to do it, it was a Heaven-sent chance. There
was something about the bachelor feeling, after those dreadful
years, that dreadful woman, poor thing, whatever you do, don't
marry too young. He ordered a large whisky, two shillings, but
who cared, drank it neat and ordered a pint of Burton and
Mild, made a few mumbling remarks and gave his quick, head-
jerking expression, like a polite man not really listening, and
went along to the sandwich counter. He ordered soup and some
ham sandwiches and started in at his paper. He peered all over
it, up and down and round about. There was nothing. It was
all right. There was nothing at all. He had another look, saw a
Standard discarded on a seat, pinched it and looked all through
it, and set to at his sandwiches. He tossed back his beer in two
gusts. There was the shadow of him on the white wall. His
head going back, his thick hands holding the tankard, his blue
jacket rather solid. His second murder, and he'd got away with
it. Perhaps the body had been found, and perhaps it was in the
morgue, but there was nothing whatever about Mr Watson in
the papers, after three whole days. He ate his sandwiches and
soup together, sipping at the brown soup, and then biting at a
sandwich. Then he ordered some more beer, he liked beer,
though it gave him a bit of a pot belly. Then he ordered a cigar.
He paid one-and-six for it. Then he went out and fumbled
along up the hill to the pub he liked called The Windsor Castle.
He liked the public bar there, it was like a country pub, there
were benches and two lots of darts going on. He sat and had
a bit of a think. He got a glimpse of himself in the mirror there
and thought: 'Well, I dunno, I think I look rather decent.'

Across the bar, a girl sat with a soldier and said about Mr
Bowling: 'There's that man who often comes in here. Doesn't
he look awful? There's something about him.'

But over in Ebury Street, Victoria, the crowd thought he
was marvellous. Queenie often said: 'Oh Lor', I'm fed up, let's
ring up poor old Bill! He'll cheer us up, and at least he's a

gentleman!' She'd get busy dialling Park 4796. She did it now and the others sat around with the Watney bottles. 'Hallo? Oh, could I speak to Mr Bowling, please? Is it a trouble?' Only, sometimes one of the other tenants answered the telephone, instead of the maid, thinking it was for them most likely, and they got snooty when it wasn't for them. 'He's out,' they'd say without going to knock.

'I wonder if you could be so kind as to give him a message when he comes in? It's Queenie Martin, he'll know. We'd love him to come over?'

... Stumbling back from The Windsor Castle, Mr Bowling went in to Number Forty and hurried up to his room. He was just beginning to feel pretty good. Regular practice during the blitz had given him a pretty good head, and all that subsequently boring time in the Ambulance Service, until he got himself invalided out with his queer heart, so it needed a good deal now to feel really good. He told himself he felt perky. He was just beginning to get the feeling of being a bachelor again, and living alone in a room in the old way which he so used to hate. A man married for reasons of loneliness, and so as to make love regularly, in his view, more often than for any other reason. Sometimes, if he was lucky, for money. If he was really lucky, he married for love. But there, some people had the luck, others didn't. He put on the light and sat on the divan thinking: 'I expect I look rather nice, sitting here, rather a quiet sort of chap, sad.' He smiled in the way he would have smiled had someone been watching who was prepared to say: 'Poor old Bill! There, there! There, there!' He started to have a little cry. He cried into his thick hands. There were so many reasons for those tears, they started so very long ago. He thought: 'I'm not a sinner at all, really. No worse than the next chap. I'd help anyone. I jolly soon started in at war work. It was partly the change, we all like change, and I got fed up with insurance. I never thought of this new line, not then. Not until we got a direct hit and we got buried, and she started up that awful screaming. And I put my hand on her mouth, close to her nose. My, she went out quickly, like a snuffed candle. It was only murder if you analysed it. There were worse things. Blackmail was worse. Homosexuality was worse. Who said murder was the only capital crime? It wasn't so in the old days. You got stoned to death for all sorts of things. Poor old girl, but she was a cow, a real cow, what a cow she was. Poor old dear. And if it hadn't been me, it might have been the roof falling in. Who could tell? Anyway, it's between me and my God.' And he thought: 'And for the first time, I got a bit of money out of something! Insurance! I'd never even thought of that!'

The maid had done the pink curtains and the blackout. He was moving to the piano when he saw the note under the door. Queenie. May as well go over, she might have some gin. He got his bowler hat again and lost no time in going out and across to the District Railway. He found Queenie and the crowd full of larks, all the Services represented, military and civil defence, and hardly room to breathe. 'Struth,' he said in his public school accent. 'No air at all! I shall pass out!'

'You pass out,' Queenie said. 'Here, dear, have some gin. I saved it.' Queenie's husband was tight and lay on the bed. He was a very boring man who had a job in the M.O.I. They all looked like him up there.

There were a pair of twins, kids in the A.T.S.

Mr Bowling thought:

'I wonder what this crowd would think if they knew.'

And he thought:

'Perhaps they will know soon. I'm doing my level best.'

But perhaps this train of thought was the gin.

CHAPTER II

BEFORE he killed his wife, which in a sense had not been premeditated, not really, Mr Bowling had reached such an intense pitch of despair about life, that he had thought of doing a murder and more or less making it reasonably easy for the police to catch him and arrest him. It was quite an honest thought, and it recurred now and then when he had had a drop of gin. After all he had been through since leaving school, all the bitter disappointments, and above all the drabness and the poverty, and his awful marriage, he had frequently and honestly felt that to get into the public eye in this way would be better than dying at last utterly unknown and exhausted spiritually. His music had failed to get him into the public eye, and goodness only knew how hard he had worked for many years, why not make a sensation of this sort? Repression, no doubt. And sex starvation. Soul starvation. Ordinary starvation, too. To hang, would at least end it and be better than suicide. And to win the appeal and get twenty years, even that would be better. Twenty years rent free and all found wasn't so bad, ask anyone who knew about these things, these years between wars? Ask them! What a joy this new war was, after the disappointment of Munich! 'It's Peace,' the placards all said. Hell, the same old humdrum, on we go as before! And then September the third. And then at last the bombs. Frightening, yes, but thrilling. Change. Who looked forward to the next peace, and the cold, starving agony nobody knew how to prevent?

He started up a coughing fit.

He swore. Somebody tapped angrily on a wall. 'Bitch,' he said. A man couldn't even cough in his own home.

Suddenly it dawned on him that this wasn't much of a home. The one thing which had made him stick his marriage was the bit of a home, it was the carpet, a nice red one. And then a direct hit, and the whole lot gone, how glad he was. Coughing, then, in the dust and mess, he'd thought, well, thank God, now a wealth of ugly memories are gone forever, photographs, books, ornaments, yes, even the bloody carpet, you can have the lot! They stood imprisoned together in a kind of black pit and she'd started up that screaming right in his ear, and he'd put out his hand. 'Are you hurt?'

'No . . .!'

'Well, shut up screaming, we're not trapped, there's a light, it's the street!' It was the Fulham street. 'See?'

But she screamed like a maniac.

It was easy to stop it.

The insurance money came to a thousand quid.

Not surprising a chap began to get ideas. And you could say it was for art?

He stumbled from pub to pub and liked to say:

'I'll get somewhere with my music now! No more worry! No more drabness! And nobody can say I've done nothing for the war? Two years in the Civil Defence? My home hit, everything gone? I've lost the lot, my dear chap, but I'm not grumbling! I'll pick up again! Watch me!'

He kept on with the firm and went to see 'the office' just as usual, and was just as patient with Mr Watson, his most self-centred client. Mr Watson depressed him very much, a dreary fellow in a brown trilby hat, with a brownish outlook. He thought we should lose the war, because he didn't think any Empire had the right to rule for more than a thousand years. He wasn't a conchie, but on his own admission, only because he had not the moral strength to face a tribunal. All he thought about was whether his money was safe, and whether his various bits and pieces were safely covered by insurance policies. He never missed a premium, never had a drink, never had a woman. He said so. It was the way he put it. Women were a sort of meal. But he was never hungry. He'd been married, but you could only imagine what it must have been like. Perhaps just at Christmas, just to cheer the old woman up.

Mr Watson lived in Fulham too, Number Ten, Peel Road, one of a row of little red houses. At the back was a row of little gardens, mostly full of potatoes and cabbages now, the war effort. Quite a lot of houses had been hit in Fulham, so that London looked like a dirty old woman who had had a lot of her teeth out. She grinned, waiting for the dentist to come back again and pull out a few more. Perhaps the dentist would come again and perhaps he wouldn't, for the present her agony was almost forgotten. The neighbours thought: 'Yes, but she looks tidy again. More or less.' Mr Watson had a married daughter called Mrs Heaton who came up from Kingston about twice a year. She wore rather cheap furs and ran a baby Austin. Mr Bowling was very interested because he knew she wouldn't get a penny when Mr Watson died, although she fondly thought she was going to get everything. Mr Watson had one day confided his will. The money was going to a dogs home. Mr Watson had been so fond of a spaniel which had passed on, he would not purchase another dog. But he liked to visit various doggie establishments, and in the parks would stop all and sundry and enquire of the owners their endearing habits. So there was *something* human about him, like there was about everyone if you searched really hard. After his wife's funeral in Fulham, and after he had got his affairs a little in order, War Damage Claim safely listed and sent in, and his furnished room in Notting Hill Gate chosen, a nice long way off, Mr Bowling sat on his divan and had a bit of a think about Mr Watson. He thought how awful he was about money, it was dreadful wanting money just for the sake of having it in the bank, better to collect fag cards, for all the good it did you or anybody else. You could forgive a decent motive. You could not forgive miserliness. It was, he confessed to himself, a little like trying to find a reason for murdering Mr Watson, but it had to be admitted he was a fair and sporting choice. If he was a happy, generous man, one would not dream of plotting against him, it wouldn't be cricket. And then, another sound reason, he'd fled from town when the Huns started coming, and crept back when the Huns had gone again. The man simply asked for it. Asked for it. He must die for Art! That was what it would amount to. His death would get a bit of good music printed and published. He would leave something to posterity after all.

He sat and tried to think about money. He was not good at it. He was too artistic, too creative, if you wanted to know. The mere thought of insurance made him shudder, but a chap had had to do something. Salary and commission, that's what it had boiled down to. 'Oh, I tootle round,' was what he explained to friends. 'See what I can pick up. What about you, old man? Your life insured? Why not come to my people?' There wasn't much in it. But it scraped up a living. Hardly enough to get tight on, though, let alone keep a wife. As for kids! 'No, siree! No bally fear!'

In his new room at Number Forty, he thought:

'If old Watson wrote out a policy saying that if he kicked the bucket he'd leave a couple of thousand quid to me, then it would be worth bumping him off. That's the ticket, I think?'

Yes, but how to make him do that? Forgery? No, that wouldn't be cricket, a chap wasn't a criminal.

He thought:

'A pot of paste. If I pasted the policy he *thought* he was signing—over the real one, allowing only the bottom for the signature? Then he'd sign the one that mattered to me, and a steaming kettle would do the rest. By jove, yes! Think it would work? Or would he spot it?'

He kicked off his shoes and lay down flat. 'I wonder,' he thought.

Mr Bowling's background was in reality so little a background at all, that to paint one at all needs a cycloramic effect. It was a colourful fusion of people in shabby places. Had they homes, it would have been a Dickensian background; but these homes were, in the main, furnished, single rooms, occasional flats. Sir

Hugh Walpole wrote of duchesses and balls and stately houses, of the hills and lakes of Cumberland. Mr Bowling had had relations with a substantial background once, but his story removed him from it as a child, and placed him, for want of a better description, with the Moderns, though not the Moderns who belonged to Noel Coward. They didn't drink cocktails, they drank mild and bitter, or draught cider when really hard pressed, and fell about Hammersmith's houses filled with it and Red Biddy. No mansion-flats for them, and less and less evening dress. They didn't go to theatres. They went to pubs and concerts, dodged or seduced landladies, and remained the people who mattered when England went to war. They knew the Labour Exchange and the Army Medical Board better than most. They had no influence, no wires to pull, and told each other: 'I hear they're taking on men, four quid a week, dear. Why not pop along and see? I know it's not *you*—but it's better than *this*?' You went along and the chap was decent, but he saw you were a gentleman and he was slightly embarrassed. He was afraid the work was dirty and rough. 'No clerical jobs, you see, they're all taken.' They thought at the Labour Exchange that an actor, author or musician temporarily a bit desperate for cash, could only fit into clerical work, and there was none. 'Would you drive a Sainsbury's van?' they sometimes asked. 'But it's hardly you, it is. I don't suppose they'd take you on.' You couldn't even draw the dole, because you hadn't been a salaried worker for at least six months. You had to queue up with the scum of the earth (which you never did) and be 'on the Parish'. Very tasty. But how different when the same government who thus humiliated you decided to go to war! 'Bloody heroes now,' Mr Bowling laughed good-naturedly at Queenie about it. 'Nothing too good for us now, what?' He was perfectly good-tempered about it. In just the same way, when he had sent in his War Damage Claim, he realised with something of a latent shock that he had lost every one of his musical compositions, the accumulated work of years. 'Why, there was a bally thing there I wrote at school, when I used to play the organ in chapel,' he laughed sadly. 'I've lost the lot . . . But, good Lor', what value can I put on them? I never had them published, modern stuff and classical stuff. They're worth only the paper they're written on—for the Salvage Campaign! Look here,' he decided whimsically, 'I'll make a present of my life work to my country, I'll claim nothing. And if that isn't patriotism, I dunno what is!' He roared with good-natured laughter and the clerk seemed rather to admire him, he hadn't liked the look of him at first, people rarely did.

'Very well, sir,' he said. 'This is the lot, then.'

'Yes. We only rented the house. I've got all I can think of in the list. Tots up to a jolly old four hundred and seventy-eight quid. And I'm not cheating you,' he challenged.

He hadn't cheated at all. He'd been warned all round: 'They aren't giving full value, you know. I should pile it up a bit. After all, remember you've got to wait till after the war—twenty years' time!'

Roars of laughter.

When they wrote and asked him to accept two-thirds of his claim, he accepted at once, regardless of genuine loss, and also the loss of his music. Who cared? There was three hundred odd quid to look forward to after the bally old war, if we won, what, and if one lived through the night's blitz. It was comfortable and one had never been fussy. Not for shillings and pence. It was the general idea of wide security, no more shabbiness, that was what one hungered for. A chap wanted something really substantial. No more of this bloody messing about. A really decent house, cottage perhaps, but in town, of course, you could have your huntin', fishin' and shootin'; a cottagey house in Knightsbridge or Belgravia, yes, Belgravia (what was left of it), or else a really decent flat. That was the ticket.

Lying flat on his divan, and plotting the demise of Mr Watson, he tried to work out how much money he must get before he could chuck the game. It was really easier to deal with one or two of his dear old lady clients, they were gullible and often fell for him, and they had pots of dough. But he was through with killing women. It had been frightful, one never thought of ugly detail. Watson was a bit of a sly customer, but that rather gave it a fillip and made it more sporting. To get him to sign the bally policy would be tricky enough, and then there was the office to think about. He would have to kill Watson the same day, or at any rate the next day, before the office could write and confirm things. And what were the office going to say? 'You're a lucky chap, aren't you, Mr Bowling? Most astonishing bit of luck, what?' Yes it wasn't going to be too simple, was it. There were mugs about, but the office weren't mugs, and Mr Watson wasn't a mug. Had he had some gin, he would have thought queerly: 'What does it matter, anyway? If I'm caught, I am! Who cares? . . . I'd rather like to be tried at the Old Bailey, honestly I would!' He heard himself assuming gin and thinking this—and wondered why, and if he really meant it deep down. Men are queer things, he thought. He whispered it to the empty room. 'Men are queer things.' Then he whispered: 'How much money shall I want, to make life real and worth while, to get stuff published, you can get these things done if you can dangle a bag of gold in the right quarters? How many must I kill?' He was vague. He thought he'd better try and get hold of ten thousand pounds, but it sounded such a large sum, when you were more used to odd ten bob notes. Money bored him and never stayed in his mind for long. Detail bored him too. It ought to be easy for the police, he thought. If they can't spot me, they'll never spot anyone. He forgot about money and the details of Watson's murder and suddenly thought: 'By jove, can I remember all my compositions? What a sweat, writing them out again? I'm not as energetic as I was.' Mr Bowling was thirty-seven. On the day he murdered Mr Watson in Fulham, he was thirty-eight. At Queenie's that same night, when she asked him what sort of a birthday he had had, he roared with laughter. But she commented that his hands were clammy.

His hands went clammy when anything really moved or excited him; it was nothing. Nerves, you called it. On his wedding day they'd been clammy, and on his first day at his public school. When his father had died, a week before that fourteenth birthday, his hands had turned clammy while he thought how unfortunate it was, now he was stuck with his stepmother, who loathed him. There were two kinds of stepmothers—which people tended to forget—the brilliantly successful, and the sadistically cruel. She was one of the latter, or he would not have criticised her for loathing him. Well, they loathed each other, there was a polite and very strained tolerance. His father had been vague as his son still was, and had left no will, so stepmother collared everything. She was a woman of 'ideas,' so she let him carry on with the public school education, but she packed him off to live permanently with a relative who had a house where the school was. She wasn't a bad old girl and was fond of the bottle. He infinitely preferred it to being with his stepmother. A severe and rather cruel snag was the enforced severance from his sister, they were genuinely fond of each other, and she was the only real affection in his life then or now. She ran away from home, married and died in childbirth, but she was as real to him now as if she was still bobbing about in the sordid world, especially when he had a go at the *Moonlight Sonata.* She'd stand by the piano, nearly enough, and he'd smile sadly at her and talk to her. Anyone coming in thought he was nuts. At school they thought he was nuts, he would do mad things, it was really in order to try and become popular, he had what was called an inferiority complex, a silly but useful phrase meaning he'd been kicked around as a child, mentally or physically, and hadn't found his feet yet; perhaps he wouldn't find his feet until he was forty or so, or at all, a chap like that naturally needed help. He needed love. It was no good sneering at it, it just showed your bally ignorance.

Well, which was worse, to have that, or to have a superiority complex? The first suited creative art quite well—you could work ferociously in the dark, without an audience and in time maybe get away with it, emerging to find your complex gone; the second suited actors and politicians, you needed all the ego and conceit you could manage—and Heaven help you if you couldn't get away with it then. At school he would do whatever the other chaps dared him, like climbing up the tower, or creeping past the Housemaster's bedroom to tap on the servant's door and moan: '*Whoooooo!*' like a ghost. When she screamed, and he got caught and flogged, he showed his marks proudly and roared with laughter. He had rather a big head, like a tadpole, and rather a pink face. The other chaps admired him, in a way, he had guts, was generous when he had anything to be generous with, but they didn't 'like' him. He didn't make a friend. He was mostly to be seen sitting over a magazine, beaming round hopefully to see if he was in favour today or not. He was hopeless at maths, good at French, plucky at boxing and swimming and P.T., a good long-distance runner, and oddly religious. His music master took a fancy to him, but it was difficult because the old chap had peculiar pawing habits with boys. It was dangerous to be up there with the bellows. 'Bowling,' he liked saying, 'you're a nice boy, I like you. You should learn to play the organ.' This he did, with easy agility, and giggling with laughter when he was kissed and fondled, it was all so silly. He composed an organ solo which was performed on Speech Day, a huge moment in his life. He beamed round at everyone that day with much success, and he heard Colton Major, a scraggy youth he had always hated, saying to his mother:

'That's Bowling, he wrote it, I was telling you, mater! He's really rather decent!'

Later, in fun, he got hold of scraggy Colton in the bushes and put a hand behind his neck and turned his scraggy frame round. It was easy. He put his hand over Colton's mouth, and rather close to his nose, and it was amusing to hear Colton's smothered screams. They were more like squeals. His face turned a dusky red, and then very slightly black. He thought he'd better let go.

Colton stood panting and gasping for breath.

'You are a . . . swine, Bowling,' he panted.

'I suppose I am.'

'. . . Why did you do that?'

'I dunno. Because we're leaving this term! Some such vague reason!'

'You are a queer fellow. I think you're a cad. You might have killed a man.'

'What of it?'

'It would have been murder.'

'Well, there's worse things than murder, Colton? Cheating. And running down a man's parents. Things like that.'

'I shan't speak to you again,' Colton panted and decided. 'For the rest of our time here.'

Bowling roared with laughter.

In bed that night he was in the dock. He was smiling confidently and the jury were looking at him, all thinking:

'He's not guilty. Can't you see—he's a gentleman.'

The judge liked him too.

But the evidence went against him, and although he and the judge had gone to the same school (he was Mr Justice Colton), he put on the Black Cap and sentenced him to be hanged by the neck. It didn't matter much, everyone knew he was not the usual criminal type, and when the last hours came and there was no reprieve there was still Angel to come and say goodbye to him, for she loved him.

Angel had lovely fair hair and warm ways with her. She was too lovely to be touched, even if you married her. You just sat at her feet, and only just dared to stroke her like a cat.

CHAPTER III

ANGEL went to the high school up the road. The boys got speaking to her over the wall. She had long golden hair and a lacrosse stick and a blue gym dress. One day Bowling trailed her all the way home, but she was too wonderful to talk to, he was too frightened, it was much safer to talk to God. So he trailed the two miles back and went into the chapel and prayed. He was afraid to pray in the proper pew, in case any of the chaps thought him a goody-goody, so he went up to the organ-loft and pretended he was about to play the organ—which he could not do in any case unless somebody worked the bellows. He felt God was real, an actual person, and that He was sorry for having to make people come down here for seventy years or so—less if you deserved it—as a sort of obscure punishment. Bowling could never see that death was a hard thing, despite all the beauties and happinesses which were to be found here; how could it be anything but a real ease from hard labour and worry, with our wars and our struggles? Yet there were people afraid of it. He honestly was not afraid of it, and he saw some vast scheme behind it all, which our inadequate mentalities were unfitted to imagine. There was some very good reason for suffering and hardship, we should probably never know what it was, we were perhaps not meant to. We just had to get along as we thought best, and try not to feel too tired after a bit. He early saw that love was the thing, marriage the nearest approach to happiness while we were here. He modelled this idea on Angel, the little girl over the wall. Up in the chapel he felt glad he had never thought or said coarse things about her, like the other chaps did, and he prayed to have somebody like that for himself. He was hungry for love, spiritual love, and loving God didn't seem quite adequate, you wanted long, feminine, golden hair to stroke. He hadn't even had a mother to love. She had quickly died. 'At the sight of you, I expect,' his stepmother had jested, a jest which hurt, as it was meant to. He grew up worried about his looks, trying to think he looked all right. He was afraid: 'Nobody will love me, I'm afraid!' That was why he smiled and laughed such a lot; hoping people would think he was nice.

'Hal*lo*,' he always said, smiling broadly. He rubbed his hands together slowly. 'Nice to see you! By jove, what?'

People were either embarrassed, or bored.

'O, good morning, Mr Bowling. How are *you*?'

Not: 'How *are* you?'

Except Queenie. She was different.

Queenie hated prudes. She's had lots of men, and was even courageous about the colour bar. She'd give you Hell if you started up that topic. She said it was just as bad as the Nazis' race creed. Humanity was the thing, we were all flesh and blood, and either our flesh and blood was feeling pretty good, or it was feeling pretty bad, and if the latter you should do something about it for folks. She got stranded for cash when she was in her 'teens and answered a friendship advertisement. 'And I've been friendly ever since,' she challenged. 'So what?' She liked to wink. 'Finally I ran into a bit of regular money and married it. So what? My heart's in the right place?'

He didn't bump into Queenie and her crowd until he was about thirty. He'd had a pretty sordid time until then. He left public school with literally nothing. The Great War—so called— was over, and now it was the bitter, workless peace.

Work? There was no work. Unless you were a factory hand, or a grocer, or a machine tool maker.

The only faint possibility for a gentleman was a frightful thing called Salesmanship.

When he was desperate, he got on to this. Writing music? 'Don't make me laugh,' he said to everyone. 'It's *who* you know— not *what* you know.' He was a fairly good pianist, but he went to agents in vain. As for selling anything!

'This won't do,' he thought, shabby and hungry. 'Is this all my education means?'

He wished he'd been apprenticed to a garage all those school years. Mending punctures and things.

He had a peep down the *Morning Post*. There was nothing. Yes, there was, there was Salesmanship. Vacuum cleaners. Trade journals. Itinerary for housewives. Doors slammed in your face, Margate, Sheffield, Maidstone and Tunbridge Wells. You could have it. There was no food in it, no clothes, no beer, no fags, no pictures, no women.

Life was complete Hell. Only those who had been through it knew what complete Hell on earth it really was, to an educated man with a sense of humour, a sense of patience, and a sense of God—which meant a sense of courage. And an artistic man, at that, whose mind and heart responded to the hidden chords of good music.

He would lie on his back on shabby divans and think about it. He'd try to laugh.

'It's no bally good giving in, you know? No blessed good at all, don't you know! What?'

He first met Queenie in a pub. It was the Plumber's Arms off Ebury Street. She wasn't married then, she was friendly. He only had fourpence, what was the good of keeping it? He'd just tumbled on to the insurance racket, commission only, and maybe things would soon brighten up a bit. He digged up the road a bit, a bed-and-breakfast place, where he owed five weeks' rent, but the old girl saw he was a gentleman and honest and down on his luck. She said openly she liked his smile and his laugh. Still, things couldn't go on like this, you know, what? He saw Queenie looking at him and smiling. He smiled too, but regretted she would be unlucky if she wanted a drink. She was a bit blowsy, but she had a nice face and a smooth skin. She used the usual technique and said hadn't she seen him somewhere before? He said the usual, yes, where was it now, but hastily adding he was flat broke, he was terribly sorry. 'That's all right, my dear,' she said at once, 'you must have one with me. Double Haig?'

'I say, doubles, eh?' he queried, wishing she'd buy a double sandwich instead.

'Why not?' she said sympathetically.

He saw her give his clothes a polite once-over.

'Married?' she said.

'Yep,' he said.

They got talking. With some people it was easy as winking. He told her about his marriage, how he'd cleared out, and how he already felt beaten and ready to go back.

'I miss my piano. And the carpet,' he laughed.

'Where?'

'Oh, Fulham.'

'Poor old you.'

'It's hers, you see. Nearly everything. It was her money when we got married, that was my big mistake. She's a lady, but she's odd. Oh, I dunno. I was only twenty-one.'

'Oh!'

'She's a bit older than me, quite a bit. Her parents cut her off, didn't like me. She drags it up. I'm never allowed to forget. She goes on and on. Year after year, you know. I dunno, at last I blew right up in the air. You have to, sooner or later, don't you?'

He laughed.

'Let's have another,' she said.

He laughed again. Very ashamed, he went pink and said, 'My dear, quite honestly, will you buy me a sandwich?'

She got half a whisky bottle, a couple of quarts of Bass, some fags, a cigar and marched him out.

'There's food at home. Come along.'

'You're a darling. This is ripping. Oh, my God, I feel a complete cad.'

'You dry up.'

'You're a perfect pet.'

'It's in here . . .'

'I wish there'd be a bally war or something, what?'

He laughed and she laughed and they stumbled up the narrow stairs to the top floor. It was rather theatreish, the hangings were like red plush. There was a not unpleasant suggestion of onions. There were two rooms, overcrowded with furniture and clothes chucked about, and the bath was in the kitchen with a board on it, the board crowded with vegetables and things. She showed the geyser, saying she'd given it a proper old polish this morning, and he could have a bath later on, just as he liked. She slipped into a white dressing gown affair and he sat smoking while she shoved something in the oven. When she finished that he gave her a kiss and they stood smiling at each other, she standing, he sitting on the edge of the bath, sort of amused, rueful expressions saying: 'This old world, what can you do with it, short of making a complete hash of it?' When he'd eaten they got talking about prudery and hypocrites, and discussing what the devil sin really was, where it began and where it ended, and what morals really were, poor old Hatry got landed, while old So and So, a complete rogue if ever there was one, remained M.P. for West Ditherminster, with packets of dough in armaments. Then they got down to whether, once agreed what sin was, you got punished for it on this earth—or later. It was very absorbing, and had always fascinated him very particularly; but Queenie dropped asleep on the sofa with his arm round her warm, plump body, and as she didn't believe in God it was unlikely they would ever reach a conclusion. Being strong as a lion, despite all the undernourishment he had gone through, he carted her into bed and got himself undressed. The effort upset him strangely, but she was dead out, so he knelt by the bed and stared at her, quaintly saying the Lord's Prayer out loud. The stuff she put on her hair was a bit faded at the roots, but she looked fair and he thought of Angel again. When he got into bed, she didn't leave much room, and he had to get out to go and switch off the light. After

that, he had to get out again twice in the night, forgetting the
light both times, so the night was like a kind of steeple chase,
treading over Queenie's plump body, and trying not to kneel on
her stomach in the dark. He made love to her in the morning
when she woke up, a sudden impulse it was, and an impatient
one, and afterwards he felt a bit worried. But she said:

'My dear boy, don't you worry about me!'

At breakfast, she used common sense.

'Be a sensible boy and go back home. You can stick it, my
dear. It's better than this? Come over and see me whenever you
get too fed up. Will you?'

He told her earnestly that he would never have been
unfaithful to his wife if only she'd played the game.

'I can assure you I'm being eminently fair,' he told her. 'I can
assure you I never thought there could be anything worse than
an unfaithful wife, Queenie. But there is.'

'Never mind,' she said. 'The Hell you know's never so bad
as the Hell you don't know. That's a true enough saying. Be a
good boy and go back. Or I shall worry.'

'It's immoral to live with a woman you don't love.'

'But you don't make love to her, do you? Be like neighbours!
Friendly enemies!'

And they laughed again.

Later in the morning, he took the tube and went home. But there
was a strange new happiness in his heart, the feeling of having
both found love and made a friend. He already felt it so strongly
that he wanted to divorce Ivy and marry Queenie. He was far
from sure that Queenie was the kind for marriage, and in any
case she had told him she would marry for security when she
got the chance, and for nothing else, she would be insane not to.
But he had been so happy with her, he was vain enough to think
he could break this down. His feelings about it were strong,
although he had got over it by evening, when he realised she was

not a lady. This was a practical thought, not a snobbish one, it was whether a gentleman could live happily married to somebody a bit different. Ivy was a lady, and look what that meant?

What a mess it all was.

He let himself in.

She was there, as he knew jolly well she would be there, and she behaved in the way he jolly well knew she would behave; she said and did simply nothing at all: she just sat around with that particular expression on her face.

Her face was pinched and had always been a bit sallow, a sort of brown that was not sunburn. There was that about her which made the name Ivy seem dry and hard and right. Her hair was black and dry. She was thirty-eight at that time, his present age, and she looked more than that. Poor old Ivy. It wasn't her fault, any more than anything was anyone else's fault. And she was every bit as unhappy. Hardly any friends, only a few callers, and cut off from her parents. It was bad luck. But they were long past the stage of trying to console one another, it had all been run through before, and was threadbare. There were deep wounds, and any words now only lead to louder words, and which made for nothing. He just let himself in, and there she was, and she sat and sewed and he wandered about. He finished up at the piano. About late evening they would have a fine old bust up, he'd have to say about the money owed to the landlady, and she'd have to fork it out; then she'd say the old one about how she always thought he was going to do such wonders with his music, and he'd trot out about how a woman ought to be an inspiration to a man, and not a hindrance. And all the rest of it. Then he'd trot out the divorce topic again, and get the usual defiant No. She challenged his religion with it, 'I thought you said you were religious?' and that was always that. Whom God hath joined together, let no man put asunder. 'We were married in church, weren't we?'

'Yes, Ivy. But the marriage has never been consummated, has it? And do you know that even the Pope is impressed by that?'

'Well,' she said then in her quiet voice, 'why don't you do something about it, then?'

'No money.'

'What about the Poor People's Act?'

'Now, Ivy, you know quite well I've applied. They refused my application.'

'There you are, then.'

'Now, Ivy, I have it on good authority they only accept a small percentage of applications, they get so many. It does not mean I have not got a case.'

Her expression continued the dialogue, triumphantly, without the need of words. He thought her cruel about it, and he was not cruel himself, always wondering what would happen to her if he did get a bit of cash together, and divorced her. Where would she go?

On this occasion, the bust up was much as usual. There were no tears, it was past that. She'd known he would come back with his tail between his legs, she supposed he was starving, she supposed he'd been sleeping with other women.

Then she slammed the door and went to bed with her Bible.

He hadn't any money to get tight with, so he played the piano furiously for an hour, and then slammed a door himself and went to bed, not with the Bible, but with a box of matches and twenty Gold Flake. In earlier days, there would have been tears from the next room. He'd have gone in.

'Now, Ivy, this won't do, my dear child. Can't we straighten this thing out?'

But there was nothing to straighten out. She just wasn't meant for men.

When he first met her—and they only met at all by the merest chance, a tragedy in itself—she'd looked so kind and well-bred and quiet, he'd fallen for her at once. 'That's the girl for me.' Her smile was a tiny bit pinched, and her lips inordinately thin, with a dark down on top, but her eyes were straight and bright, they were dark blue. It wasn't Angel, but it was perhaps Angel with dark hair. He'd been taken to a musical show by the aunt he stayed with during his school days, not many months before the old girl died. She was to meet a friend at the theatre, and when they got there this friend had just bumped into a Mr and Mrs Faggot, and their daughter. 'This is our daughter—Ivy.' They'd made a party of it, getting the seats changed at the box office so they could all sit together. And if they hadn't just chanced to see the Faggots, he would never have seen Ivy. But there, wasn't history made up of these ifs? He and Ivy seemed to have got on fine. He hadn't fancied the old birds much, but you couldn't get on with everyone. 'No, I've got musical ambitions, really,' he confided in Ivy in the interval. 'Not this kind of thing, I'm afraid. The more's the pity. There's money in it.'

'Classical?' she asked, sounding interested.

'Well, yes. I'm not saying I spurn the other. That will sound young. But I want to write. And play, too, of course.'

'The violin?'

'No. Piano.'

They went to several concerts, and one summer night at the back of the Albert Hall he discovered she'd never been kissed. She was rather shocked at being set upon in the street, so to speak, but he laughed.

'You mustn't mind, Ivy. What other chance do I get? Your people watch me like a pair of hawks, I'm afraid they don't approve of me at all.'

'Yes, they do,' she lied.

'Well, won't you kiss me? I mean, there's nobody about?'

'Don't be so common, William. I know you aren't common, but we oughtn't to behave like servants.'

He laughed.

'Why not? If we don't feel like servants?'

Their very first row was when he slapped her bottom good-humouredly, never a habit of his with ladies, but solely in an effort to make her a bit more human. To his astonishment, she turned pale with anger and humiliation and fainted. When she came round, he couldn't help laughing because, if she wanted the truth, she never let him touch her anywhere else. He laughed and told her.

The first shock of realising she literally knew nothing, was a pretty stiff one. Victorian novels and all that, he thought. And he thought of her stiff and starchy and exceedingly stupid old mother, and felt no longer surprised, only angry. Poor kid.

'Look,' he sat on the bed and said, 'Don't you worry, old dear? I'm not a lout, I'd simply no idea, honestly.'

He could see she believed him, but she was too embarrassed to do anything other than huddle in the hotel sheets, like a wan and rather too old fairy who has just been assaulted by a hitherto virtuous gnome. 'Look, Ivy, we'll just talk. Or, shall I clear out? Whatever you say, my pet? I'll dress again and go for a bit of a tootle by the sea, what?' They were at St Leonards, of all Godforsaken places, The Hotel Criole, a fearful affair up the hill. Her mother had known of it, needless to say, and practically insisted. The old crab. But he'd laughed—you knew what that kind of woman was. 'Whatever you say, Mrs Faggot!'

'It is what my daughter says, I should hope,' the silly cow said. My word, to think that kind of person lived safely through her seventy years and then died comfortably in her bed.

But he laughed.

'Hastings,' Ivy confirmed, so Hastings it was, at least, they seemed to call it St Leonards down there, though it looked all one to most people.

It was a bit of a job explaining to Ivy, in one's best public school manner, where babies came from. She seemed to know, and yet she didn't. She vowed she *did* know. 'Of *course* I do, Bill, but . . .!'

'But what, my dear child?' he smiled. 'Silly old thing!'

She sniffed and sobbed.

'Never mind. Don't even think about it,' he said kindly, he

went out of his way to be kind and considerate for months and months. 'It's quite unimportant,' he pretended.

When he decided it was time to stop pretending, they were in the half-house in Blythe Road, Fulham, a basement, ground floor, first floor affair, some other family living upstairs. The marriage was already gravely threatened; quarrels, hair falling out in the bath, and other nervous disorders too despairing to mention, he thought. It dawned on him that he ought to have seen Doctor Elliot about her ages ago, though Dr Elliot was usually too fuddled to be seen about anything except elbowitis. But he tootled along and tackled him in the saloon. 'Look,' he said, 'confidentially, old man, I want to talk to you about the wife. She's driving me balmy.' He laughed, being slightly embarrassed, but old Elliot wouldn't send a bill in, this interview would only cost a pint of bitter, eightpence.

He returned home quite jubilant, and although they'd had a bit of an Upandowner in the early afternoon, he was very kind and considerate.

'Ivy, my dear,' he said gently, sitting beside her. 'I've got this for you. I think we might save our marriage even yet.' He gave her the admission card Elliot had given him, to a local hospital. 'Will you go? You will, won't you? It's your duty, surely, isn't it?'

She gave one look at the card, coloured, swung round and gave him a fearful welt round the face.

He got straight up and walked out of the house.

His face was hot one side, cold the other. His heart was icy cold all over, all round inside and out. Bloody Hell! Women. Well, well! there was something to be said for homosexuality after all. He was through with women. Through with them? He'd never started with them. Merely married one of them, one who wouldn't even go to a hospital and be examined, perhaps have a small bit of an operation. This was the end.

He strode about Kensington Gardens, not knowing how he

had got there, but realising slowly he hadn't the fare back and must walk, in shoes which let the snow through.

The park looked sad and nice. It was white, the trees were stark and white, and the people like cold, uncertain shadows, moving about the ice of the Round Pond.

The sun was blurred red and shapeless up there in the grey-black of more snow to come, it looked like a half-healed wound.

When he got back, his feet were wet and cold and he was worn out. He was too tired to say any of the things he had decided to say. What was the use of saying he was going to leave her? Where would he go? Where would she go?

And what would God say about his obligations?

What God might not say about hers, were not his affair. He was full of self betterment, and spiritual theories, and liked to feel that marriage led two people towards a goal.

What could he feel now?

She sewed and she said:

'I'm sorry I lost my temper. I ought not to have done that. I apologise.'

This time it was he who sat and said nothing.

She said:

'You must realise, William, a woman is different, physically, mentally, and spiritually, from a man.'

'I do begin to realise it,' he said quietly.

CHAPTER IV

THERE was a fearful shindy the first time it came out that he had made love, as she called it, to a girl who came in to dust up the old homestead. She was a naughty little thing, and he found her methods irresistible. In vain did he tell himself he was not playing cricket, and he loyally refused to allow himself to think: 'It's entirely Ivy's fault.' It wasn't. It was his fault, and it was Elsie's fault. Elsie was sixteen and her trouble was she had elder brothers. She kept getting in his way in the passage, and smiling up at him and going red. She had a floppy little body which it was impossible to ignore. When Ivy cleared out Up West one winter afternoon, he went up to Elsie, who beamed round and upwards, and, as she put it later, 'Let him take a liberty with me, but I didn't mind, at least Mr Bowling is a gentleman.' On the bed, there was no difficulty about clothes, because the wretched child didn't seem to go in for them. She had soft lips and elegant teeth and Cleopatra appeared to have nothing on her. And although he condemned himself for a cad, and thought about the old school and all that sort of thing, he repeated the performance at teatime, and many teatimes afterwards. It was a bit of a strain, craning the neck up at the basement window, to see if old Ivy was coming up the road yet. And needless to say the poor child clicked, as she called it, dead on the three months to the minute. This at least threw off a certain amount of reserve, and they went at their love affair hammer and tongs while the going was good. His health at once recovered, he liked women again, thought about Angel, and even contemplated marriage with dirty little Elsie. This didn't last long, however, and he started in at insurance with new zest, now and again varying it by crowd work at Elstree, whence his accent very occasionally got him a line to say, or his dinner jacket got him a sitting part in a cabaret scene. Then he came home one day and heard, smelt and saw the fat sizzling in the fire. He couldn't resist:

'Well, my dear Ivy, you've asked for it, you know, I must say!'

Needless to say, she said:

'How like a man! You're a cad and a brute, and I hope you go to prison!'

'Prison?' he said, startled, and had quite a turn when it became apparent Elsie had lied about her age, and was really only a pullet-like fifteen, or had been 'at the time of the alleged incident'. This was going back a bit, and he did some anxious arithmetic. Elsie stood about, sniffing and sobbing, and looking more like a slut than she ever had before, as if to increase his shame, and he thought: 'Well, now perhaps I've achieved a divorce, which will be something!' But not a bit of it. There was to be no freedom, and the threat of prison hovered for some time, together with the unpleasing rumour that Elsie's dad, from the docks, was coming along presently to tear his block off. Unnerved by the general prospect, he hurried along to Queenie, confessed all, and was well ticked off for his lack of caution. However, it was worth it, for she took on her shoulders the entire matter, going to fix up for Elsie where she was to have the baby, firmly insisting that she got it adopted immediately afterwards, and the outlook began to look a little safer. Life with Ivy was then grim indeed. She threw it up at him for each meal, and she threw his music up at him, 'not that you do any,' and she threw money items up at him, 'not that you earn any.' They had frenzied scenes, and slammed doors at each other, and hated the very sight and thought of each other. Sometimes he went to the piano in a state of exhaustion, and composed a sad little tune which he knew was rather good. But when he saw music publishers about it, they just smoked cigars at him, said nice things, but were clearly thinking about something totally different. One winter he got a nice little job playing in a concert party at Eastbourne, but something or other happened, a quarrel or something, and he was soon back picking up the crumbs from insurance magnates' tables.

'I dunno, I'm sure,' was what he thought about life. And he laughed helplessly. 'I dunno, I'll tootle along and see old Queenie. See if she's really going to be married.'

Having had a good time with old Queenie, and learned that she was going to marry a crashing bore because he had a fiver coming in certain, apart from his job, he went out with the quid she pressed down his shirt, and had a couple at Victoria Station. He returned home to Ivy and silence, read a bit of *If Winter Comes*, the only book in the place, and chain-smoked in bed with it.

Life crept by, Ivy got older, he felt now older, now younger, and wondered what on earth the whole thing was about. Why be born a gentleman if you weren't allowed to live like one? It was the most frightful punishment in the world.

He felt this most when he had to visit the office. He always sensed that it was resented. When he finally got on the salary list up at the office, he felt his particular department resented that too. Apart from the manager, who was usually too important to be talked to, there were only two blokes who concerned his little affairs at all, Mr Nash and Mr Rosin. They were two beauties. They both had hilariously witty things to say about his old school tie, and about Lord Baldwin and Mr Chamberlain. The things they had to say somehow seemed to appear to be Mr Bowling's fault. Mr Nash was thin and sour, and Mr Rosin had a flat, stupid face like an uncut cheese. The really common man, Mr Bowling decided, was a nice chap, but these two belonged to the half-and-half species; they were really sprung from the common man but they thought they were old school tie whilst resenting that sorry class. They loved it when a public school man got sent to gaol, and took care to cut the bits of news out of their paper for when he next came in. 'There you are, Mr Bowling,' they pushed it forward, winking at each other, 'there's your old school tie for you. H'r! H'r!' too stupid to realise that at any moment he could cut out a bit of news about Winston Churchill and say, 'And there *you* are, Mr Rosin, and Mr Nash, there's another of your old school ties for you! H'r H'r?' But a chap wouldn't stoop to it.

Coming in to collect the thousand quid, Messrs Rosin and Nash had appeared very different, almost admiring.

Such was the pitiful power of filthy lucre.

'Money, money,' he sighed time and again. You just could not ignore that miserable subject.

It was tough if a chap was bad at it.

He liked to ponder upon the illogical, in respect of money. You got paid for doing what was called 'a job,' but which was often and often nothing but sitting around. But for real hard work, like thinking out and writing something, more often than not you got Sweet Fanny Adams.

And they said when you had got money, you thought about it even more—in case you should lose it.

It was true of Mr Watson, at any rate.

The day he murdered Mr Watson, he got up early. Thinking about it had deprived him of a good deal of sleep, yet he felt a kind of exhilaration. He'd pasted the policy carefully on top of the other one, and it didn't look too bad. There was the ridge at the bottom, of course, which old Watson would at once spot, but he'd explain to him: 'Paper economy, old chap, if you don't mind?' and Mr Watson wouldn't mind, because he liked to try and give the impression that he was doing something for the war effort, it was so obvious he was doing nothing. 'All right,' he'd say. If he didn't, the deal was off. Something else would have to be thought out.

At breakfast, Mr Bowling felt a bit restive. He was a man of leisure, these days. He'd eaten into his thousand quid a bit, nothing much, but a bit, it was so nice being able to give old Queenie bits and pieces, after all her kindnesses when he was down. He gave her a nice bit of cat, thirty quid it cost, and she was so pleased. She kissed him and he laughed: 'Just a bit of cat!'

'And you be careful who you marry next time, my dear,' she told him. 'Come and see me first!'

And he'd thrown a bit of a party, here at Number Forty, yes, with the bombs still whistling down, you only died once, didn't you. There was a din, and he played the piano and they sang, and the chap came down from upstairs to complain. He played about with chemistry or something of the kind, he'd been to Oxford and he was interested in Mr Bowling. He was a bit of a bore, that first day stopping him in the hall downstairs.

'My name's Winthrop. Alexandra Winthrop. I hear you're joining us.'

'Yes. Bowling's the name.'

'Miss Brown was telling me, Mr Bowling. I hear you were blitzed. Bad luck! Yes, she told me about it. I'm very sorry.'

'Oh, well.'

'You mustn't be lonely. I'll pop in, may I? And you must pop up.' He frowned. 'Usually busy. Eton?' he guessed.

'No.'

'Ah. H'm. Well, I shall hope to see you. Bath water's always hot,' Mr Winthrop informed, and went out with a friendly nod.

Mr Bowling went up to his room. He didn't want to know any of these people. Winthrop already seemed to know about Ivy having been killed.

He frowned and shut the door, wondering who else lived in the place.

With the plans forming in his mind, he preferred solitude.

On the day of Watson's murder, Winthrop knocked at the door and came in without waiting. He smoked his pipe and wore a Norfolk jacket.

'Ah. H'm. 'Morning, Bowling?'

Mr Winthrop was just a lonely and middle-aged man. And he was a bit inquisitive.

He chattered and peered about. He was already insured, so

he was sheer waste of time. He gave peeping looks all over the shop. He chattered about the furnishings here being better than most places of the kind, said Miss Brown was a dear, 'she's a lady, you know,' and remarked that Mr Bowling seemed to have made a lot of purchases, suits and shirts, and said he believed there would very shortly be coupons for clothes. He said it must be awful to lose your things, and he said the various things he thought about the Ambulance Service, the Home Guard, the Fire Service, and the F.A.P. He swayed to and fro on little brown shoes, but looking overweighted with fat. His face was round and his mouth disgruntled. He was a flabby man. He said all about the people who came to live in the house, they changed weekly sometimes, but that Miss Brown preferred people to stay, providing they were, 'gentlemen like ourselves'. He dragged Mr Bowling up to his 'den', which appeared to be a square room with a wide view of blitzed London, and crammed with wires and cables and acid bottles and chemistry books. When he got out at last, it was eleven o'clock, and the strain of being civil to Mr Winthrop had made him nervy. With his policies, he went along by bus to Fulham, for his interview with Mr Watson. On the bus, he thought: 'Is this I who am doing this? Am I really going to do this?' It was certainly quite a nice bright morning for a murder.

He no longer thought he was going to do it at all.

He'd just go along.

'Good morning, old man?' he hailed Mr Watson as he went up the little tiled path. Old Watson was in his doorway looking up at the sky. He was looking singularly well and alive. His grey moustache was very neat and trim, as if he was back from the barber's.

'Oh,' he said, 'good! How are you, Mr Bowling? Haven't seen you for some time. Sorry to hear about your little affair.'

'Oh, well . . .'

Mr Watson had a habit of chewing some real or imaginary

morsel, as if the last meal had been singularly pleasant and recent. His eyes gleamed, while he did it.

He kept his caller in the little porch for a time, talking about various things, how he didn't like the Welsh, and how he didn't really like the English much either, and then jumping from that in a mentally restless manner, to geraniums. He pointed at various green plants in boxes, as if Mr Bowling was sure to be fond of flowers, never mind whether they were in flower or not.

Mr Bowling kept going.

'By jove, really, how interesting,' when being told about various bugs which ate leaves and so on. 'Well, I'm blowed, what?'

'I spray them,' Mr Watson went on, endlessly.

Mr Bowling was wondering whether Mr Watson's teeth would be likely to fall out, they might get to the back of his throat, and choke up the epiglottis. It might not look like murder, then.

The conversation veered round towards the blitz again.

'Yes,' Mr Watson said, 'I was very shocked indeed to hear about your poor wife.'

'Oh, well . . .'

'I know what it's like. I lost my wife suddenly one Saturday afternoon,' he said, rather as if he'd taken her shopping, and it had happened that way.

'Really?'

'A bus . . .'

'I say! I'm sorry, a beastly thing, that!'

'But these things happen! Sad! Sad! But we've all got to go sometime.'

'That's true enough.'

'Well, now, come into the dining room. There are various things to go into. And I expect you want my signature.'

They went into the dining room. It was very neat, and there was a picture of Mr Watson's married daughter sitting in a deck chair at Margate and showing the most hideous legs. She really looked a corker. There was a plant in the firegrate, and on the table were Mr Watson's pens and bits of blotting, all very fussy and neat, everything at right angles to everything else. He was like an old hen with his things. He sat busily down in his salt-and-pepper suit and started frowning about his money and his policies and his views on the Stock Exchange in general. The moment he saw the policy Mr Bowling had planned to try and get him to sign, he seized it in his bony fingers and stared.

Mr Bowling got to his left side, a little behind him.

'Whatever's this?' Mr Watson exclaimed. 'This won't do at all,' he said, and suddenly tore it up into little pieces.

He turned round towards Mr Bowling as if for another form, and Mr Bowling put his thick hand out. He suddenly and rather thoughtfully put his hand on Mr Watson's moustache, and pressed Mr Watson's head back so that it rested on his own chest, and the chair tilted and came back, and he quite easily dragged Mr Watson backwards out of sight of the little bay window. He felt the back of his legs touching the red plush settee, and he allowed himself to say quietly: 'Take it easily, then it won't take at all long,' to Mr Watson, whose expression, if it was possible to judge it, was that of a startled child being forced to play a game he had never played before, and didn't really like.

Mr Watson poised in mid-air, on the tilted chair, but generously supported in every possible way by his companion, over-toppled the chair, which fell on its side with a mild bump. Some footsteps went up the road, and some footsteps came down the road.

Mr Watson had started to do extraordinary things with his hands. He seized Mr Bowling's two ears, and contrived to give a very sharp and fairly prolonged twist to them. After that, he transferred his grip to Mr Bowling's hair.

When that had but little effect, he started up a bit of a spluttering, covering Mr Bowling's hand with spittle, and managing to grip in pincer movements at the backs of Mr Bowling's hams.

There was quite a strong smell of geraniums, Mr Bowling noticed. It was not unpleasant. He thought several times: 'What is actually happening? Am I dreaming?'

If he was dreaming, the dream continued.

The red plush settee again touched the backs of his calves. Mr Watson was frantically trying to get freed by a rapid series of shakes. He shook his stomach to and fro, and wriggled. Mr Bowling permitted himself to sit and get a better purchase, as it occurred to him that Mr Watson might be going to take rather longer than Ivy had. Mr Watson's grey eyes began to show a neat mixture of astonishment and increasing terror, and he wriggled and spreadeagled his long pepper-and-salt legs, and managed to get a bit of breath in through his nose. Mr Bowling tightened the vacuum there, and pressed hard at the moustache, which was a trifle ticklish. Mr Watson's attitude was a trifle obscene. Various things began to pass rapidly through Mr Bowling's brain, which had begun to be astonishingly clear. He thought, well, this was rather amazing, he hadn't wasted much time, so he was doing it after all—and why? There was no money in it, none whatever: now, why was that thought such a comfort? Why? Why, because, one supposed, fraud was rather a shabby thing; even if it was money belonging to a company worth millions, it was still fraud. And another thing, did it occur to one that somebody else may be at that moment in the little house? In the kitchen, perhaps? And another thing: where did one get this method from? It was pretty effective. Burke and Hare used to do it. Had one *read* of it first, or *thought* of it first and *then* read of it? The subconscious was a very interesting thing. Did people realise that places were sometimes haunted by the future—as well as by the past? Did one . . .?

There was no stopping the amazing pace of his thoughts. His life raced backwards and forwards. He was holding Colton behind the chapel. Now it was Mr Watson again. Now it was poor Ivy.

Now it was Mr Watson.

Why was it? Why was he doing it? And why did he now know he was going to do several more murders? Murders? Don't call them that—such a vulgar word.

Then it came to him swiftly and clearly that he was doing it because he was so thoroughly disappointed in himself and his life; *he wanted to be caught.*

He wanted it.

Suddenly Mr Watson managed to give a violent lurch.

But it didn't mean anything. His face was black, his head had sunk, his body gave a kind of twist and Mr Bowling held him a few moments more and then allowed it to collapse face downwards into the red cushion. He pulled up the sagging knees and dumped them on the settee and stood up. He was panting.

Presently, Mr Bowling straightened his collar, took up his papers and hat and went out of the house.

He smiled in the summer sunshine and decided to go to the pictures.

He went to the Metropole in Victoria, somehow he felt more at home in Victoria than Fulham, it was near to Queenie, where he would go later on. For the present, he wanted the quiet and the dark, but not the quiet and the dark of solitude.

He wanted to think things out.

He presently decided that he was a fox. He wanted the chase, he expected to be caught, and he even wanted that. He wanted the hunters to have every chance.

He was one of life's misfits. A bungler with money, and with life; just a poor devil with an artistic soul, ruined by education. Cursed or blessed with a weak heart, and thereby useless to his country in matters to do with killing; just a knock-about. Yes, yes, he thought in the pictures, the sooner they catch me, the better: though not a soul will ever understand. Not a soul.

He sat in the pictures with his eyes shut, in very severe mental agony.

Half way through the big picture, he fell fast asleep. When he woke up, people were roaring with laughter. He roared with laughter too until tears came.

Then he slipped out and hurriedly bought a newspaper.

CHAPTER V

QUEENIE was waiting for him in the new flat she and Rodney had recently chosen. They still stuck to Belgravia, it was a habit, it was home, they knew all the locals.

Locals were their background.

Queenie was wife-hunting for Mr Bowling. 'Dear Bill,' as she called him. 'I must have a scout round,' she told Rodney in her pleasant way.

'I doubt if you need trouble,' Rodney said. He took what he called rather a poor view of that Bowling fellow.

'Whyever?' Queenie teased him now and again.

'I hate cynics,' Rodney commented, and he argued with Queenie that there was too much of the cynic about that Bowling fellow. She wouldn't agree, saying that 'old Bill simply wants understanding.'

'Maybe I don't understand him, then!'

'And he's going through something,' she frowned. She was vague about this, usually tossing it aside with a laugh.

Rodney liked to say that Bill had been rather rude to him about the Civil Service being what he called 'departmental minded', licking each other's boots in a time-serving way in the interests of advancement, and afterwards running each other down behind each other's backs. All individuality, Mr Bowling pronounced, was unhesitatingly sacrificed in the interests of pay day. On top of this, that fellow Bowling had got a bit tight one night and it had got back to him that Bowling thought him 'typical' of the M.O.I. If you offered yourself for a war job there, (Bowling reported) they put you through an exam, and only when you passed it suddenly thought of asking you about your grade of health. If you said you were Grade One, Two or Three, they said, sorry, can't employ you unless you're Grade Four, old chap, and looked brightly at you, almost proud of the waste of time and paper involved in the preliminary correspondence and the exam! And Bowling had said: 'The perfect job for dear old Rodney—suit him down to the ground.'

Queenie seemed to side with Bowling and was an extraordinary staunch champion of his. She was vehement.

'My dear,' she laughed, 'you just don't know him! He's as honest and open as the day. According to his lights! Which is more than one can say for some—I don't mean you, you old pencil!' She often called him an old pencil, because of his work at the M.O.I. She teased him about being a pencil and a bit of paper. 'Try and be nice to him, won't you, darling. He's had a tough break. Married too young. No cash. This time he must try and marry a bit of money, it's the only thing for a man of his temperament. There's no shame in it, it's logic, and he's got music in him.'

'He's not very good looking, is he?'

'Hark at him! And nor are you! You old pencil!'

'I mean, he always looks as if . . . as if he's acting a part. As if he's out of his sphere.'

'He is out of sphere. The poor lamb. He ought to live on his country estate. Or somebody ought to leave him some dough and a title. He'd probably do wonders for charity and write a symphony or something.'

'H'ar!'

'I'll give you h'ar, my sweet. You lay off my boy friend. He's thoroughly sincere. *And* decidedly religious, we've had some rare old talks in our day. I wonder if Doris would like him. She's pretty. And kind. Bill ought to have somebody a bit maternal.'

When he came in, she noticed that his hand was clammy. She thought he was nervous about Rodney being there.

'My word,' Bill said, staring round at the new place, 'this is pretty posh, what?'

Rodney Wellington saw him come in. He thought he looked

what he would call well dressed. Sports jacket and grey flannels,
well creased. Bowing slightly as he shook hands, suave manners,
perfectly poised. Thin fair hair slightly grey, nicely done at the
left side, white cuffs showing a bit. He looked like a rather nice
schoolmaster. And yet that something a little . . . grotesque?
His head was queerly shaped, barbers must be fascinated; not
unlike a rather neat mangold wurzle? And that colour in his
face—an over-pink: like a man who drinks whisky secretly and
to excess.

But he didn't do that, did he?

Sorry, but not possible to like him as much as Queenie does,
oh, educated, granted, not the Varsity, but . . .

'How are you, Rodney?'

'How do you do? Glad to see you!'

Liar, thought Mr Bowling, but laughed pleasantly at something Queenie said. He suddenly felt a whole lot better. Normal
again. It had been a dreadful afternoon. Black, black depression.

Doris came in.

A whole crowd came in. It was a big flat, and suddenly Mr
Bowling was saying to Doris that he wanted one like it. Why
live in a single room, for pity's sake?

Doris was nice. She was perky and liked to show her taut
little figure. She wore a permanent broad smile and was well
dressed. She'd been on the stage, in films, on the radio, in
shops, in clubs as a hostess, on an airliner, and was just going
into munitions. They made no particular contact of any kind,
beyond a mutual curiosity. She had decided she would like to
sleep with him, and would do so if he asked her. But he astonished her later, after poker, by telling her he saw no happiness
in promiscuity, and was against Free Love. She felt very
surprised at first, but then, looking at him again, was not so
surprised. There was something sincere about him, as Queenie
had said. He was bright and didn't seem the moody kind,
though you couldn't possibly tell that at a first meeting. He

looked at her once, rather sadly, and although they never met again, she remembered him for a very long time. She said to Queenie after:

'You don't often meet an interesting man. I liked him.'

. . . When he got home, it was late, and there was not the need to tiptoe upstairs for fear of being bored by someone; old Winthrop would be safely in bed upstairs surrounded by his acid bottles and cables and chemistry books: old Miss Brown, doubtless with her floppy hat on, for he had never seen her without it, would be asleep in one of these rooms downstairs, he was never quite sure where she hung out. Alice, the maid, would be in the basement with the cat.

He chuckled and went up to his room. Went in and took care not to put the light on, he had left the windows open and the blackout down, despite Alice's protestations. Alice liked to cart her bulky form round the place doing all the curtains and things, or the police started ringing the bell 'and it upsets Miss Brown.'

He fumbled about and undressed in the dark, dropping his clothes vaguely on the floor. He stood on one leg by the open window, smelling the warm night, it was pitch dark, he couldn't see any stars. The slow footsteps of a policeman on patrol came up the road, stopped, came on again, dwindled slowly away again. And he thought:

'The sooner they come for me, the better. Yes, the sooner the whole bally business is over, the better it will be. The feeble mess I made with that paste and policy! I'm just not cut out for a crook. Always be yourself, that's the ticket. I wonder if they've spotted poor old Watson yet, and I wonder if I left a clue behind. I hope I left something. It'll make an interesting trial, all his bally affairs in perfect order, nothing missing? You realise, my dear chap, with his face stuffed into that cushion, some old doctor may think he had a heart attack and suffocated himself? Or can they tell? Probably they can tell a thing like that. They're so darned clever these days. Finger prints? I

daresay I left one or two. They'll be sure to come to me, somebody probably saw me going along to his little house, or coming
away from it? Poor old Watson, hope it wasn't too unpleasant,
no desire to hurt anyone, but it hadn't taken very long.'

He hopped about on one leg, pulling off a sock. He got into
his pyjamas and got into bed. Alice had turned the bed down,
these rooms were better than most, distinct attempts at comfort
and refinement. All the same, the great idea was to get a nice
furnished flat like Queenie's, three or four rooms, then one
could have a few of the folks round, cards, or some music.
Tomorrow slip up to that flaming insurance office and say:
'Sorry, old boy, I'm chucking the insurance racket. Going back
into Civil Defence, or war work of some kind. Time I did.'
Messrs Rosin and Nash, unless they'd been called up by now,
could have his little clientele. Also, they might have news of
Watson. 'I say, Bowling, one of your clients pegged out
yesterday. Have you been told? Old Watson, Peel Street,
Fulham.'

'Oh?'

'Yes.' And perhaps they'd say: 'Murder, Bowling. What can
you make of that? The poor blighter got strangled or something.
The police are there now.'

Perhaps they'd say:

'Ah, there you are, Bowling I think a Police Inspector's
wanting to see you. When did you last see Watson? Somebody's
snuffed him out.'

He put an arm out to the radio and switched it on, thinking,
yes, I suppose I've got about eight hundred quid, that'll be
quite enough to last me till this thing is through. Of course, it's
a form of suicide, really—but a darned interesting and sporting
one, it'll give an exciting run whichever way you look at it.

But when he went to the office next day, nobody said a word
about Watson, or about anything; even about old school ties.
They were one and all bored to death with his news about

leaving insurance, too many of the firm had left already, what was one more?

'Well, cheerio,' he said vaguely, and thought: 'My God, to think I stuck you all for so long, miserable lot of . . .' He went down in the lift and stepped out buoyantly into Holborn and shouted for a taxi. What a joy to yell for a bally taxi. He charged cheerily back home to see if anything had happened in any form about old Watson, but nothing whatever had, it was exceedingly uncanny. It occurred to him the old chap might stay face down on that settee for weeks. Surely the postman or milkman have kicked up a shindy by now? He felt rather upset. It interfered with his plans. What was the good of going into a new flat if one was going to be arrested in a day or two? He went to bed, got up, played the piano, went in the park and sat in deck chairs in the sun, went to the pictures, saw Queenie, and pub-crawled for three more days. Nothing whatever happened in any shape or form. One morning he woke up in a good humour and there was a letter forwarded to him care of the office. It was from Watson's daughter at Kingston, and he laughed aloud, both with humour and suddenly relief from strain. She 'regretted to inform' him that her father had 'had a seizure' and the funeral was yesterday. 'He was quite all right when the charwoman came at ten, and at eleven she went out to do the shopping. She was not gone more than twenty minutes, and when she came back he was dead.' This gave him a considerable thrill. The charwoman might have come in any second, and caught him. If that wasn't giving the hunters a sporting chance, what was? '. . . But what I am really writing to say is did my father ever say anything to you about his will, I want to contest the will, for I fear he may have been out of his mind, for he has left every penny to a home for little dogs, I thought I could perhaps get evidence concerning his state of mind, and I know he liked talking to you. It would be nice if you wrote, and of course my husband and I would be only too glad to remunerate you for any trouble you took, I enclose a stamp. It seems very hard, doesn't it, because we were devoted, and I have this house to keep up, and the little car, and times are very worrying. Yours sincerely, Fanny Heaton. P.S. I shall await your reply with anxiety, and so will my husband, who sends his kindest regards.'

He roared with laughter and shouted: 'Bitch,' and reached out to the radio in time for the eight o'clock news.

He got out of bed and started his breakfast arrangements. The idea here was to cook all your own stuff, and to go out and do little bits of shopping. Sometimes he wheedled Alice to cope with it all for him, but she appeared to be busy today. The news said we had brought down a lot of 'planes, only losing a third of the quantity ourselves, and that Russia had also, and that our recent shipping losses were only a third of the enemy's. After the news, there would be a talk on interesting ways of cooking rice, and tonight and tomorrow there would be talks by a Pole, a Slovak and a Norwegian on what they had for breakfast in their own country. While his bacon was frying, he switched over to get some music, and one way and another his breakfast hour was enlivened by *Handel in the Strand, Molly on the Shore*, and the news in German, which he followed more or less, thinking: 'German's just like English. Quite astonishing.' And he thought: 'Spoils one's selective taste, all this choice of programmes, at all hours of the day and night.' He felt in good form. There was a new mood of relief. After all, it was only fair that a fox should have a bit of peace between hunts, and be at leisure to relax from the panorama of beauty and ugliness and moods: the mood which transported to the heights, and the mood which brought you down the muddy hole to ruin. One was still a fox, a rather pleasant thing to look at, well trimmed, but really only a menace and a blot to the face of the green and yellow earth.

He sat in sudden dejection, again sorry that he was free to go on as before.

It seemed that God didn't want him, even in this poor way.

. . . All over England, statelier homes and houses sat about long tables, having breakfast handed to them on silver trays.

'Fried liver, Sir William?'

'Why, thank you, James! I think I will, what?'

'And the car is waiting at the door, Sir William.'

'Thank you, James!'

The city and the hearth. The ministry and the hearth.

Home and children.

Religion, the future, grandchildren.

But in London the days began with the dreary scream of a smelly bus. The radio said:

'Well, now, any workers who ought to be thinking about the factory, or some similar destination, I ought to remind you that it is just coming up to six minutes to eight. Meanwhile, here is Bing Crosby singing *Take Me Back To My Boots And Saddle.*'

Mr Bowling thought:

'Well, I shall shove in to the new flat and chance it. I must have a bit of a think.'

He was sitting sadly in his red dressing gown when Alice knocked and came in with a large plate of bacon and two whole eggs, some toast, real butter and a spot of real marmalade. Her shiny face beamed at him.

He was halfway through his breakfast, but he smiled politely at her for her kindness, and winked when she said on no account to tell Miss Brown, and finally he pretended he was still frightfully hungry, and allowed her to set the dish down before him. When she stooped, she made rather a daring business of kissing him on the bald bit on his head.

One day in the hall he had made the fatal error of giving her a kiss, he'd been in a jubilant mood about something or other, some trifle, and she was a dear old thing. But it had been a fatal error of judgment and appeared to have unloosed the last bonds of love which bound her in her fading age.

She liked to hover now, in a portly, starchy and speechless

manner, red and ugly in the face, with dry, protruding lips, such as he disliked, love was in the lips, if it was anywhere, you could kiss your way to happiness, or recoil from lips to something quite different. She looked like the Nurse in *Romeo and Juliet*, but she thought there was still time to be Juliet just once more; and she clearly thought he was Romeo. It was awkward. In another sense, she looked as sinister as Lady Macbeth. She had endearing habits with policemen, and could be seen in the shadows of the square outside, leaning up against the railings in the arms of the law. If you walked down the road and didn't come back for two hours, they'd still be there quite motionless. What did she do now that the Government had removed the railings? It was a serious thought all over England, he mused. Had the Government made any provision? Could such apply for a special war bonus?

The only thing to do with her was to banter her, and make a fearful joke of everything, and to hope her duties would quickly call her from the room. The trouble was, she hovered. There was just that bright smile, that you-are-a-one gaze of loving admiration, and that habit of tidying up the room. She never said much. 'Your *room*, Mr Bowling!' Or: 'Your *clothes*, Mr Bowling, *tch*!' And she'd wink and tidy up everything. Her false teeth slid about rather. She said she liked his suits, the blue one, the grey one and the brown one. She said she liked his bowler hat best, and not to wear the felt, dear. And she said she liked him in striped pyjamas, decided this was a cue for a wink and added something else.

'Now, now,' he bantered, embarrassed, 'you're a naughty girl, Alice! At your age!'

Beams.

'How old do you think I am, then?'

'Older than that copper I saw you with last night. Who were you with last night,' he chanted, shaving, 'Oh, *who* were you with last night! I can't think how you manage it, standing up, what?'

Her shiny face turned beetroot.

'Oh, get on with you, Mr Bowling! That's not like you to make a remark like that!'

'Sorry . . . !'

'What a thing to have said!'

She rustled out in her starch, and he knew she was delighted. When he was having a snooze one day she crept in and was rather a nuisance.

'Now, now, Alice? Won't you ever grow old?'

Her face shone like the sun and she sat on the bed.

'You're the nicest gentleman I've ever had to look after,' she said. 'And that's saying something.'

She just sat and beamed.

He thought then, as he thought again now:

'Oh, my God—I shall have to get out of this!'

Just then Mr Winthrop knocked and walked in without waiting.

Alice didn't like him and hurried out. 'He tells tales to Miss Brown,' she pouted about him.

CHAPTER VI

MR WINTHROP took up a position by the fireplace, and was anxious to know whether Mr Bowling would like to come upstairs and have some coffee with him and a few friends next Thursday. He said that was in three days time, and he said they would have an awfully interesting time, and he knew he would not be bored, and the coffee was from his aunt in Sussex, whose husband had been a coffee planter in Ceylon. He asked Mr Bowling if he would join the Home Guard, you only needed to turn up once a week, and then when Invasion came you had a definite job to do. He said all the chaps were decent blokes, mostly city, though he was afraid some were 'mixed up with the stage', an item which caused him to frown, and to start swaying to and fro on his little brown shoes as if he was the Leaning Tower of Pisa. He looked flabby and boring, and apropos of his remark about the stage, suddenly confided that he was married, and that his wife was on the stage, 'or she was when I last heard from her.' Then he frowned away from that, and rattled on, 'sure I'm not boring you?' about what he would do if he was Minister of Supply, and what he would do if he had five minutes talk with Stalin, and what he would do with Japan and the Generals over there, and how he would advise President Roosevelt. The entire time, he was completely unaware that one of his more important buttons was undone, a detail which would have robbed each and every one of his interviews of all dignity and consequence. So far from being amused, however, Mr Bowling became suddenly aware that there would be no party upstairs for Mr Winthrop on Thursday and that in that case it was safe to accept the invitation. A black, black mood had descended upon him, and he sat trying not to glower at Mr Winthrop's button. Mr Winthrop, completely unaware of how very fateful his intrusion was being for himself, leaned to and fro and tried to run the World War and bring it to a successful conclusion for democracy and freedom, and of course Capitalism.

'What *is* freedom?' Mr Bowling heard his own voice querying. He was looking out of the window.

In the pretty square, a little girl and a little boy were playing on the grass with hoops. Mr Winthrop peeping out at them, portentously drew a neat illustration, explaining that what we were fighting for was so that the little girl and boy could go on playing with hoops, and so that, in due course, their own little girls and boys could play with hoops in their turn, instead of being slaves and working in a pit or at a lathe for a Nazi controlled world. He went on and on and on, and it was all quite good, but Mr Bowling was no longer listening, his vision transcended far beyond Mr Winthrop's present vision, and he saw the slavery which the world endured, even when it had got what it fondly called freedom—the slavery of the soul forcibly tied to the body.

'With Ivy,' he thought, 'what could ever be a greater bondage, than the bondage of those days?'

There were a thousand forms of slavery, under the title Freedom; ought the title to be improved? and it might be that under the horror of slavery, there was much freedom, beauty and rest. This was frightening, it needed thought. And where, then, the happy medium?

Mr Winthrop had all the arguments, of course. It was all quite good, and all that sort of thing. But it was all rather hackneyed and sickening.

'My dear chap,' he said gloomily to Mr Winthrop, 'if we win this war, which I know now we will, what happens? Why, we're right back where we started from.' His black mood descended and he longed for the shadows of night and wondered what exact time old Winthrop went to bed. Had he a mother and father?

'I often wonder,' Mr Winthrop went on and on saying, 'when I think of these appalling atrocities, what kind of precautions it is possible for the people to take? When they know the brutes are coming, I mean. The women and girls, I mean. Such things do not bear thinking of.'

'All things must be thought of,' Mr Bowling said despondently. 'In the matter of living. And dying.'

Mr Winthrop thought:

'A queer card, this chap Bowling. Depressive. Don't think he likes me.' He blew his nose and said: 'Ah—music?' and went to the piano. He started to play and sing *Sigh No More Ladies*, in a voice like a eunuch.

Mr Bowling sat stock still looking rather thoughtful.

He sat there for an hour after Mr Winthrop had cleared out, saying:

'On Thursday then, Bowling? Shall we say eight o'clock? Can't possibly provide food, with this confounded rationing— but nobody expects it these days.'

'I shall have eaten.'

'Splendid! You play bridge, of course.'

'Yes and no.'

'We'll have to see. Hope you won't be bored? We can chat.'

He gave a pull at his pipe with wet lips and smiled not too comfortably and backed out. His pipe smoke lingered behind him, blue, circular, wafting towards Heaven.

Mr Bowling sat solemnly staring around the room. It was nice, yes, and it had atmosphere, there was taste here. There was the open window, the smell of grass, the smell of tar, the bright squeals of children.

But in the room were a hundred ghosts.

Ghosts of a hundred men and women and girls who had hired this room before; the lonely, the hungry, the wretched, the frightened, the suicidal, the rapable, the mean, the happy.

Eyes were here. Eyes which may have thought of the far-off

days of mother and home, and who now stared in fear at the gas fire, the little brass pipe leading to the tap of it, and thought in fear of God:

Dare I?

Perhaps the contented stared here too—but how could you be contented here?

No, the atmosphere was post-modern here; it was spelt in five letters: *worry*.

The marks of their heads were on the wall, at the head of the divan. They had sat there writing letters. 'Dear Sir, In answer to your advertisement in today's *Daily Telegraph*, I am of public school education, aged thirty-eight, can speak French and a little German. I . . .'

Mr Bowling sprung to his feet and decided he couldn't stand the place a day longer. He must have been out of his mind to have come here. But then you acted according to the circumstances, mood and decisions of the time, didn't you? Something prodded you from behind, and you jumped.

This time he jumped into the bathroom. He would wash this place out of his skin, find a furnished flat and live in comfort for the remaining time Fate placed at his disposal. It was unlikely that it would be long.

While he bath'd, the door handle was tried four times. The bally house seemed to be full. Alice had said it was empty, but one supposed the cautious felt it safe to return from the country towns.

He had little idea who lived in the house. He had seen women coming in and out, and a tall chap with a bald head; and another chap who wore a little straw hat.

By tea time, he had found a furnished flat which was down the hill, a threehalfpenny bus ride. It was in a modern block oddly out of place with the rest of Addison Road. He fell for the flat at once, it was on the fifth floor, you could see houses and gardens and Shepherds Bush Green, and pubs by the dozen. It had been newly painted and the hangings, such little as were needed, were new. There were three large rooms, a kitchen, a bathroom which was a joy, and a little balcony to sit out on and have your tea. The owner was in Ireland on a war job. The furniture was yellow and modern looking, the cupboards and lights were in the wall, there was plenty of glass and crockery and sheets, and there were two yellow lifts which you worked yourself. He was so excited that he noticed everything and noticed nothing. The only snag was that the manager was sorry but he could not come in until next week, they were having the drains up. He went out into the street and felt like a violent walk. He enjoyed a perverted kind of outing, walking vigorously the whole way to the gap which had been his home with Ivy, there was the mirror still stuck to the wall, where he had shaved time and time again, and had shouted round at Ivy: 'Oh, for the love of Mike, my dear child, will you stop nagging? Well, really, Ivy, you drive a chap balmy! Honestly!' They'd cleared up the mess at the bottom, and there was the now-earthy gap where Ivy and he had fallen in that black minute, and, shocked, it had come to him that, of all people who ought to be allowed to die, it was himself, with perhaps poor Ivy as runner-up; but no, the likes of them had to survive a direct hit which must kill the two lovebirds upstairs. For them, they must carry on in the old way; and she must scream, on with the bloody motley, and he must cry in customary anger: 'Are you hurt?'

'No.'

'Well, shut up screaming, then.' And then his hand on her mouth in the darkness there and the choking dust.

And then the sound of fire engines.

And then the sound of sliding timber and brick, a crash or two of slates; and the feel of wetness at his knees and feet, and the feel of her poor, unhappy body slipping down at his feet in supplication; she'd been released at last, this was *her* freedom.

'I've set you free, Ivy! My poor child, you're free, my dear? Good luck, my dear? I hope you get a better break next time? . . . Goodbye, Ivy, my dear?'

Suddenly tears blinded his eyes. Why in God's name did he come here? He'd be going to Watson's next!

Suddenly he started running like a madman down the dirty road. 'Taxi? . . . Taxi? . . .'

In the taxi he lay back flat, like a poker. Had he seen his face, it was pale and drawn.

He looked sick.

But he sprung out lightly and was outwardly himself when he knocked on Miss Brown's private door and went in to give a week's notice.

He felt as if he was drugged. Watching himself talking to Miss Brown, who was at tea in her hat and surrounded by photographs and prints and paintings and ornaments, and talking to a nurse who wore a wide smile and a pretty blue bonnet, he heard their voices, his own and the two women's, and the lawn mower outside, and the milkman, and a horse and cart.

'This is my niece, Mr Bowling. Miss Brashier. She's at King Charles's. Will you have a cup of tea with us? I'm *sorry* you can't stop just for a cup . . . ! You may speak before Miss Brashier, you don't mind, I know, Ivy.' Ivy! 'Leaving us, Mr Bowling, oh, now, I really am disappointed, and so will dear Mr Winthrop be, he was telling me all about you.'

'Yes, well, I want a bigger place and . . .'

'Poor Mr Bowling got bombed out, Ivy. It was so sad.'

'I *am* sorry,' Miss Brashier's voice said. She said it well, considering the number of such cases she had had to deal with, and the number of time bombs she had known were whizzing down in the yard outside the ward window. 'But let's hope those times are over! They say our air defences are marvellous now!'

He went upstairs, forgetting all about dinner, and all about alcohol, and sat playing some Brahms quietly for a very long time. It got darker and darker.

Mr Winthrop's footsteps started to come up the stairs. Mr Bowling heard them pause outside his door, hesitant. But no knock came. The steps started to go on up the winding stairs towards the noisy cistern there.

Mr Bowling leapt to his door like a cat and softly opened it.

Mr Winthrop groped for the light switch at the top of the narrow stairs, and tried not to make any noise, in case of waking up Miss Hull, a new tenant on his floor. She went to bed early, he knew, and got annoyed if the radio was on too loud.

He thought he heard a slight sound behind him, and he paused.

Then he thought he heard somebody breathing.

The next thing he knew was the uncomfortable sensation of a hand coming at him from behind and gripping his nose and mouth. His own hand had reached for the light switch, and found it. But very quickly indeed did he withdraw it again and tear at the hairy hand which now held him in a suffocating grasp. He at once thought of burglars, and didn't care at all how much they stole, so long as they let him breathe. He felt himself being pulled a complete but slow back-somersault; there was another hand at his chest, he presumed it was fishing for his wallet.

Mr Winthrop started jerking and twisting. This was getting beyond a joke, his lungs were bursting. This intruder was most inordinately strong. He twisted and turned, pulled and pushed, and he felt his body hit the bannisters and the wall, and gradually his body assumed a prone position, heavily weighted, and with head pointing dizzily down the stairs. He kicked, but his feet hit nothing. They both slid downwards for a few stairs.

It now came to Mr Winthrop that this could not, after all, be plain burglary. It was something extremely different. His lungs were at bursting point, and his two hands had no further strength with which to tear at those merciless hands which had started to blacken him out. He prayed. But one gasp of air and he'd let out such a yell which would wake the already dead.

But there was no gasp of air; only a black, suffocating silence, and the sound of heavy and dreadful breathing, which he envied.

Mr Winthrop then knew that he was going to die. He immediately said in his mind:

'Oh, Vera, my dear, you must forgive me? I've behaved very badly to you, I know it, but I'm paying for it now? If only I could finish the letter I'd actually started to write, it's on my table now. Please believe me . . .'

His thoughts broke and dissected into a thousand fragments, only Vera remained, good to him to the last, as she always had been. He was now in very great pain, he was at the bottom of the sea, though quite dry, and the weight of the sea was too great for him to rise to the surface and breathe again God's beautiful air, and smell the cannon smoke in it. In a moment, it would be over, his head would explode, and he could sink down, down, down, he could rest.

His body began to go limp.

Feeling it slacken, Mr Bowling felt a relief. He didn't want the poor chap to suffer unduly. Mr Winthrop's body went limp and they both slid in the darkness a couple more stairs.

Suddenly a door opened somewhere. There was a long, long pause, and he imagined somebody listening. He waited, breathing heavily and quietly.

Then the door quietly closed again.

He felt Winthrop's heart and there was no movement. He got up. He left him face downwards there. He went down the stairs to his room. When he approached his door he was startled to see a light. He had left it pitch dark, the blackout wasn't up. The police would be in any second.

He charged into the room and suddenly stopped.

'Hallo!' a girl said. She said: 'I did the blackout. You look hot. Have you been having a bath?' She smiled and sat down.

He took out his handkerchief and wiped his face. He lit a fag and said fairly calmly:

'I thought you'd left?'

She giggled and said something about being back in the room next to him, and how it was like home. The silly little thing was suddenly serious about it all, saying some nonsense about it being love, and she didn't realise it until she'd gone. Lighting his cigarette, he'd noticed that there were scratch marks right across the back of his hand, as if the old cat had done it. He immediately thought: 'I'm for it this time, they'll find bits of my skin under his nails.' He got a sense of the hunt. May as well give them a run for their money.

'Got any iodine, Joan?' he said. 'The damn cat.'

She ran down to the bathroom cupboard and back. All the time the house was still as the graveyard. Mr Winthrop lay where he had left him, alone in the shadows, waiting for the very first person to go up or down those stairs. It might be Miss Hull if she came down to the lavatory in the night, or it might be Miss Brown on the prowl, or most likely of all it would be poor old Alice in the early morning.

He put out his left hand.

'You couldn't have been having a bath, it's not steamy in there? Why were you so hot? Oh, your poor hand, Bill, what a beastly scratch. Where is the cat now, darling?'

She dabbed on iodine and chattered, never waiting for an answer. He thought: 'I shouldn't have bothered about the new flat.'

He got out some whisky.

CHAPTER VII

'Here you are,' he said. 'And then clear off to bed. There's a sensible girl. I'm tired.'

But no, she would have it she was going to stop. He had only seen her a few times before, when she'd been in the room next door. He'd come in and she'd be just coming out of her room, or out of the telephone kiosk. The second time, she asked him in for a sherry, and of course he'd asked her back one night and given her a glass of port. She'd been a bit of a nuisance that night too, and two or three days later. But he'd held out good-naturedly and sent her packing.

Nothing would shift her now. She behaved like a kid, slipped off the blue thing she had on and jumped into his red bed. She giggled and sat grinning at him enquiringly with her knees hunched.

'No,' he said good-temperedly.

'Oh, Bill,' she said, and put out a thin white arm and shut off one of the two lights.

She snuggled down. She had great coils of yellow hair and it was like a shower of gold on the pillow. But there was nothing to it, he thought, no heart, no brain, only a rather flat body which probably needed washing. She had quite nice pyjamas, that was about the only thing.

And yet, it was not unpleasant, her being here just now; he was more and more nervous of loneliness. Used to it, it yet had grown to a sensation almost physical, when it caught him. It soon drove him to Queenie, or to the street, or the crowded public bars where people screamed and spat. She was lonely too, that was her trouble, it was most people's trouble, in some form or another; either you were Joan, and very lonely, or you

57

were King Charles and the loneliest man in the world. Or you were stuck in Berchtesgaden, longing for a street café and just one real friend to talk to: you couldn't even talk to God.

They had a bit of a wrangle. She had long, tapering fingers, and all sorts of ideas and promises. But he got up and began to arrange a chair at the foot of the armchair. 'I slept like this at the ambulance station,' he explained, 'so I may as well do it again. And I only had a deck chair there.' He settled down after he had put the lights out and removed the blackout for some air. It was sweltering. She started up copying the noise an owl was making outside the window. He settled down and made the same row himself. It was very ridiculous. Poor old Winthrop upside down and dead out there on the stairs, and the two of them in here laughing and going:

'*Too-hoo? Too-hoo?*'

'I'm still at Smiths,' she chattered. 'Have you read much lately?'

'I gave up reading,' he said with his eyes shut, 'during my marriage. My dear, misguided wife considered that books only made for dust. I shall have to start again. Perhaps that's what's wrong with me.'

'There's nothing wrong with you.'

'Am I mad?'

'Mad! You!'

'But *am* I?'

Her voice had a young, musical lilt to it. Perhaps she had a bit of Irish in her somewhere.

'Mad? I should think you're the sanest person I know. And the nicest,' she said quite seriously. 'D'you know what I think's wrong with you, Bill? You're too much alone. Why don't you marry me? Then you'd have a home again. You're the kind of man who's lost unless he's got a home and some kids. You'd make a wonderful father.'

He laughed dreamily.

'Family life built the nation! True! And it will probably build it again when this conflagration has burnt itself out . . . But not for me, I greatly fear . . . !'

'Yes, you fear—why do you? It'd be the making of you!'

'My dear Joan, has it occurred to you that one must first love—and be loved?'

She leapt out of bed and knelt at his feet, encircling him with those long, white arms. In the darkness, he imagined her round face turned up to him, and her rather long breasts which he remembered seeing freely on a former occasion, and he sat dreamily to listen while she said:

'Don't you see, Bill—I love you, really I do, I could make you happy, life would become full, instead of empty, it would be so worth while?'

It was hopeless. He told her she'd drive him mad in a week, you built a marriage on something far deeper and more solid than anything they could ever bring to it. Besides, you needed money, a man did. He hadn't believed that once, but by gum, he believed it now. She sidetracked all about how her people had pegged out, and all she'd had was this job at Smiths. She thought somebody ought to write a book about 'people like us', and he assured her hundreds had, and hundreds more would, 'so get to bed and go to sleep, there's a good child, I'm tired!'

'I could write a book about my life, Bill! Really I could! And when I see some of the stuff that's written!'

'Dry up. Go to sleep.'

'Not unless you come to bed too.'

'Why don't you go back to your own room?'

'It's drear and loathsome and I hate it. I want to be with you.' She sat in silence and then wondered: 'I suppose you have lots of affairs. Of course you do.'

'I don't believe in affairs, as you call them.'

She had seized his hand and was trying to pull him up off the armchair. Without effort, he pulled her down and pretended that she was poor old Winthrop out there.

He laughed and soon let go.

'Don't, Bill,' she giggled, 'I could hardly breathe! What enormous hands you've got! They're like steel . . . ! Come on, darling, to bed.' She pulled at him.

At last, he said:

'Well, I give in, as usual, but no funny business.'

She quickly nestled down in the crook of his left arm, showering his face with gold. He chewed it contemplatively, reaching firmly to seize her two hands and hold them still. 'Shut up and go to sleep.'

'Oh, Bill . . . !'

'You're a bloody nuisance,' he said good-naturedly. 'You'll never get a man with plaguesome methods. You should learn to be rude and cold.'

'That method's dangerous,' she said interestedly. 'Too many men take it as meant.'

'Well, you have a try,' he said. 'Give it a trial. I give you my word you'll be married in six months.'

'I do wish I was married,' she said.

The clock ticked.

Big Ben struck midnight.

He thought: 'It'll be foul play, this time. That's quite clear. Scotland Yard will take it up. Question the house. Well, I spent the night here with Joan, that'll put her in a slight spot. Wonder if I dropped anything by the body? A button? A thread? Trifles like these hanged you, didn't they? And then the man's nails. And the scratch on the back of my hand, with iodine on it, and Joan coming in and saying, "You look hot. Have you been having a bath?" No, there was no steam in the bathroom. The cat did that.'

Where was the old cat last night? Perhaps it had been run over the day before yesterday?

He saw himself sitting in the dock. Well groomed; caricaturists making hay while his star set. Reporters putting: 'His refined accents and educated appearance obviously impressed the jury and the court. His charm of manner, and his apparent sincerity, coupled with the lack of motive, make this one of the most interesting and sensational trials on record. Miss Brown, in the witness box, said she had never known a more charming and . . .'

But it made no difference. There was his very flesh under the nails of the deceased, the girl Joan, the scratch and the iodine, the cat had been run over the day before.

With tears running openly down his cheek, the foreman of the jury sentenced him, in effect, to death. The evidence was conclusive. The judge, in fact, sentenced him to be hanged by the neck until he was dead, he was to be taken to the place whence he came, and thence to a place of execution. The *Evening Standard* placards would shout: *Public School Murderer To Hang!*

And what did it mean? Why, it meant happiness! It meant, in fact, *freedom*.

'I did it for freedom,' he might risk telling Queenie, when she came along for the last interview. 'My own freedom,' he'd give a rueful little laugh. Her kind, agonised face would stare across the long table at him.

'Oh, *Bill* . . . !'

Poor old Queenie!

The warders would be very decent fellows. They'd play whist and chess and realise that he was a cut above the usual murderer, not in character, but in cloth. They might even let him lock the closet door; and trust him with a razor, or his old school tie.

'He's a sport,' they'd say. 'Darned if I think he did it?'

The chaplain would be ripping. He'd come to intercede for him on behalf of God. 'I want to set your mind at one with God's,' he'd say excitingly. 'Shake hands, won't you, Bowling?'

He'd reply:

'Why, that's just what I want, old man!' and he'd grip his

hand warmly. 'That's just the bally thing I want! It's what it's all about!' And he'd sink down on his cell bed, head in hands, and sincerely mean it, just as he'd sat through so many unhappy nights and days on shabby London beds, thinking and meaning it, and trying to puzzle it out. 'And then I got bombed,' he'd tell the parson. 'But God didn't want me even *then*! I decided I'd *make* him want me. Do you *see*?' And if by chance he didn't see, at least he'd see his sincerity and agony.

And then at last there'd be the last scene of all. A rope and a handshake and a bit of pain. He'd stand stiffly on the square, wooden platform.

What was a short pain like that, eh, Winthrop, Watson, old man? Ivy? What was it, compared with all the suffering here, the horrors of peace and war, chiefly peace?

And then face to face with the Lord Himself.

A huge hand, his own, made of hairs and steel, pointing out challengingly, as well as pleadingly, to God, who had power of us all.

'What have I to say? . . . What have I not? What *need* I to say? *Thou knowest all!*'

And his expression would change like the shadows on the wall of fading summer, green, yellow, red, like traffic lights; stop, now you can go; stop.

A sound of thunder, like the thunder which had come after the Crucifixion. A tremendous thundering.

He started out of his dream with a cry and sat bolt upright.

Somebody was thundering on his door.

The early morning light was filtering mistily in.

Alice rushed in.

'This night shalt thou be with me in Paradise' had been the veiled, misty words teasing his brain while it slept, and he remembered a parson chap telling him how those words only really meant that Barabbas would be with Christ for that actual night, and it did not mean what public school education taught you that it meant, to wit, that the sinner Barabbas had achieved, in his sin, what Christ had achieved in His suffering and goodness, and had attained the complete Heaven: *for that actual night only*; while Christ would go on to the complete Heaven. It was interesting, and his brain wanted him to go on with the dream but the thunder and panic started in, like men with a tree trunk swinging at the Gates of Hell to open them for him.

Alice's face was a kind of mottled white. She looked as if she had first of all turned ashy white, then reacted to a deep, dark flush, then gone puce. Her dry old lips were working, and her bovine eyes were wide with fright.

Even in her panic, she caught sight of the threads of gold hair which he was trying to hide under the sheets, and he saw the spasm of jealousy which flitted like a shadow of vexation across her kind old face, as with his other hand he held Joan down, yet she wriggled and said in a stifled voice:

'What's the din . . . ? *Bill . . . ?*'

Anger and jealousy were chased away from Alice's face by a spasm of shocked disgust, and she was herself again. 'Mr Bowling, could you come, sir? Something dreadful's happened . . . Mr Winthrop . . . !' She put a handkerchief partly into her mouth, to steady the flood of tears which waited in obedience. Alice always cried when anyone was dead, and, if it looked fishy, she had to look scared like this. The clock downstairs started to chime seven. Somewhere or other, through a wall, a familiar voice said this was the seven o'clock news, and it said who was reading it.

He had a bit of a job with old Winthrop. He was lying head downwards on the narrow stairs there, and his arms were out at a ridiculous angle, as if he was spouting a spot of Shakespeare in his sleep. Alice was afraid to touch what she called his 'poor, dear corpse,' and she looked as if the sight of Winthrop's face was going to make her sick. Miss Hull heard the din they made, and came out in a sort of turban affair, wearing protruding, startled eyes and a pinched look, and smelling of some vine-garish lotion she liked to put on her grey hair. She wouldn't touch Winthrop either, and he had to go downstairs and knock up a chap Alice said was called Mr Gunter, on the second floor. He knocked and a sleepy, startled voice said, hallo, in a surprised way, as if nobody had ever called on him in his life before, and that it must be the police for certain. Mr Bowling went in and was at leisure to see that Mr Gunter slept without pyjamas, and without his teeth in. It took a bit of time, so he stood and waited while Mr Gunter's ginger coloured body was clad in striped trousers and a brown jacket, and while his teeth were rescued from their smiling position in what looked like a glass of saline solution. He told Mr Gunter that he was fright-fully sorry to disturb him, but the poor chap upstairs had kicked the bucket and fallen downstairs or something.

Mr Gunter covered his queer looking nipples with his brown jacket, and looked scared stiff. Mr Bowling wondered whether he was scared at being seen with nothing on, or at anyone knowing he hadn't got any pyjamas, or at the hearing of some-body having died.

'I *say*!' he kept saying, buttoning up everything. 'By jove, how frightful . . . !'

'I can't lift him by myself. And the women are nervous.'

'I say, though! dead, eh?'

They went upstairs, Mr Gunter's mouth being half open, and his face half pale. He kept going: 'You mean he's actually *dead*?'

'Now, then,' Mr Bowling said.

They got Winthrop up to his room and put him on his bed. His arms remained in their grotesque posture, with his head twisted back at a strained angle. His legs were twisted inwards and there was a stain down there.

On the writing table, Mr Bowling noticed a letter which began and tailed off.

'My dear Vera,

'I have been wondering what to reply to your last letter, and I have decided to split my answer into two parts. Firstly, my dear Vera, I want to explain my . . .'

Dear, oh, dear, Mr Bowling thought sadly, what a tedious letter it must have been going to be!

He said sadly and softly:

'I'd better go down and tell Miss Brown. And we'd better get a doctor. Mere formality, of course, but there it is.'

He slipped out.

Alice, Miss Hull and Mr Gunter stood in a group staring at the body on the bed. Alice was now sobbing unrestrainedly and saying how fond of him she had always been, which was the silly sort of thing the dear old thing would be expected to say in the circumstances.

Miss Brown awoke from a gentle dream about yellow jasmine growing on the garden wall at home, and dear father sitting in his deck chair there smoking a Turkish cigarette, and heard the pleasant, educated accent of that delightful Mr Bowling saying apologetically and very tactfully:

'I'm terribly sorry to intrude upon you, Miss Brown? Are you awake? I'm afraid poor Winthrop passed away last night . . .'

Mr Bowling stood at his frying pan and became aware that a sensation of excitement pervaded him. He regretted it, deep within himself, because he did not feel it was sporting to enjoy any sensation at the expense of poor Winthrop; but, he thought, hang it all, a man could not prevent inner emotions which rose from subconscious reason.

It was the emotion of the hunt. The hunt was up; if the end of the hunt was as grave as he hoped and expected it to be, perhaps he was entitled to the present sensation of excitement, while it lasted.

Strange voices were in the house, and strange footsteps had

gone up the stairs. Joan had come in twice, to whisper a kind of panic, she greatly feared old Alice may have seen her in the bed with him, and as she told Miss Brown everything, she felt rather worried,

'Why worry?' he commented vaguely, and turned the rasher over.

'Because she'll make me leave,' she cried, vexed. Then she went out again.

Alice came in three times to say wasn't it awful, and to say Dr Gilestone was here, and to say Dr Gilestone had gone, and to say he hadn't made any remark at all about the cause of death, but he'd looked grave.

Miss Brown came in, with her hat on, to say how terribly sorry she was that her tenants had been disturbed, and that she did so hope Miss Hull wouldn't give notice, she was looking rather pale.

He poked thoughtfully at the rasher. Mr Bowling's kitchen arrangements were a sort of cupboard with four shelves high up, and a cooking stove midway, balanced on top of a small refrigerator. There were two of everything, cups, saucers, milk jugs, basins, spoons, forks and knives, and the frying pan hung up on a nail as a rule, as did the saucepan now. There were strong bacon fumes which charged across the room and out of the window. He usually stood to eat, because to sit at it meant crossing the room to the little round table, which had a habit of collapsing, and then you had to start all over again from scratch. If it didn't collapse, then you forgot something, and had to trail miles back again to get whatever it was.

In another corner of the room was a brown screen, behind which you could wash with running water, though you couldn't possibly shave, on account of the mirror being too low and giving you a crick in the back, and it being a sort of glazed brown on the surface, and it being so hung that any light there was fell slap across the back of your own head and blotted out everything.

He stood eating and deciding:

'I'll shave in the bathroom today. That bloody mirror.'

And he wondered what the shaving arrangements were like in prison. Did you go to the Scrubs, or where was it nowadays? Pentonville?

And he thought with a sigh:

'The sooner it's over, the better!'

Then he stood rather still, listening.

CHAPTER VIII

He was standing washing up when the knock came.

He went quickly to the door, holding the dish cloth with the red stripe, and the white cup, and wearing on his face the expression of anxious concern how-is-the-patient-now sort of thing, and seeing the police officer there, though in plain clothes he looked the complete copper, put on his face the look ah-worse-I-fear-I'm-so-sorry.

'Hallo, old chap,' he said, quietly as at a funeral.

The policeman's expression changed within seconds of seeing Mr Bowling. He looked in that state of mind which says:

'Oh, I say *Sir* now.'

'Good morning, sir.' he said, and sounded apologetic.

Mr Bowling said in grave tones to come right in.

'Thank you, sir. It's just about the unfortunate matter upstairs, you know . . .'

'Quite, quite.'

'Only,' the copper said, 'the doctor won't sign a death certificate, and as there'll be a post mortem, we've got to make a few enquiries.'

Mr Bowling looked extremely grave and shocked, and the copper said who he was, and produced a picture of himself in a wallet which looked like a passport. The photograph, Mr Bowling thought, was exceedingly good and flattering, and felt constrained to say so. He laughed.

'Not that one should joke at a time like this,' his laugh faded. 'But it struck me.'

The copper laughed softly. He looked about twenty-one, but must have been more than that.

*

He said he'd just got to know who was in the house last night, and so on. Mr Bowling said he fully understood, and he said he was in the house the entire evening and night. He said why wouldn't the doctor sign a death certificate, and was told that Mr Winthrop had been smothered.

'*Smothered?*' said Mr Bowling.

'We are wondering if any outside agent could have got in. Or if he had any enemies.'

'I couldn't imagine him having any *enemies*,' Mr Bowling said.

'Very likeable and interesting, I believe.'

'Quite a good chap.'

'A great friend of yours, sir?'

Mr Bowling said Winthrop often came in for a chat, and had actually been in only yesterday morning to invite him to bridge on the Thursday next, and he'd accepted.

When the copper went off to question somebody else, Joan slipped in again with some ridiculous talk about wondering if the police thought she'd murdered Mr Winthrop.

'You?' he said.

She was scared and she said:

'Well, they think it's murder. Personally, I should think it was a housebreaker or someone. I can't imagine Mr Gunter doing it, or anyone else here? And Alice says they think he was killed last night about eleven or so, that was just when I came into your room and you were . . . or I thought you were having a bath.' She stared vacantly. 'Where were you?'

'Walking,' he said, and burst out laughing.

She hurried on with the news: 'So in case they thought it was me, I said I was in here with you all the evening, and stayed all night! I don't care if Miss Brown is shocked, I don't suppose she's a virgin either.' She slipped out, frowning anxiously.

His face fell.

When the detective returned and said: 'I have to ask you if you were alone last evening and last night, sir, I'm sorry to . . .' he replied sharply:

'Why shouldn't I have been alone?'

But the fellow suddenly winked.

'As a matter of fact, sir,' he said, 'Alice saw her come in here! Though she wasn't sure of the time!' He winked again and went out.

He sat and stared in front of him, anger rising.

Alice? Prowling about and watching his movements? Well, what else had she seen, perhaps? There was a grave discrepancy of about four minutes or more?

Emotions battled within him; one minute he saw that the police would never even suspect him, and he felt pleased and superior: the next minute he felt sure that Alice would give him away, she'd seen everything—and he felt resigned and dejected.

He sat and waited.

It had begun to rain. It was a nice summer rain and it brought down the first brown leaves with it. It hissed sleepily on the tarred road outside.

Nothing further happened and the house seemed quiet.

Alice came in at teatime. Her face was red with crying, and her eyes, which were puffy in any case, looked like Cornish pasties. He was having his tea and he thought, now we shall hear something. When do they come for me?

But she said, pouting:

'I hope you're ashamed, Mr Bowling, taking up with a hussy like that! I saw her slip into your room last night, I was doing the curtain on the landing down there! I never thought you'd take up with a hussy like that, sir,' she half complained, half teased. 'And then when I came in this morning and saw her in your bed? . . .'

She pouted, head on one side.

He stirred his tea despondently, thinking wearily:

'If this mare doesn't clear out of it I think I shall vomit!'

'Do you hear, Mr Bowling?' she teased in a motherly, thick-skinned way.

He smiled good-temperedly.

'What do the police think?' he said. 'One doesn't come across murder every day.'

The word brought her to her senses and her handkerchief came out again.

'*Murder*,' she said in tones of horror. 'Only to *think* of it!'

He smirked.

'Good Lor', why make so much fuss, Alice? Murder's a very over-rated word. It's the fault of fiction. We don't squirm about in horror when we hear a king has been murdered, we call it assassination and get on with our breakfast. But when Mr Jones crowns Mrs Jones, probably because she richly deserves it, we call it murder and rush and stare at her miserable little house! What is the matter with us all? If old Winthrop's been murdered, I daresay there's a good reason for it all somewhere? People are being murdered all over the world this very moment in a revolting and often brutal fashion—but we can only hope that there's a scheme of things behind it all? See my meaning?'

She chewed her handkerchief and said rather coyly she thought he was callous about Mr Winthrop. It was a tease.

'Callous? Why only the other day, Alice, you told me he was the biggest bore you'd ever met! If somebody's smothered him, then they've done you a good turn! I believe you smothered him yourself!'

Her hands flew up.

She cried:

'Oh, *there*, Mr Bowling, how *can* you, *really*?' and her face went mottled.

He was thinking:

'That detective must be as balmy as the doctor who examined old Watson! What is the matter with people?'

He said slowly and quietly to Alice.

'Will you let me confide in you?'

Her face lit up. 'Confide in me?' she said hopefully.

He leaned forward.

'I smothered old Winthrop myself,' he said quietly. 'I was in here, and I heard him standing outside my door. He didn't come in, and I heard him going on upstairs to his room. I crept after him, Alice, and, just as he was reaching the top stair, I pounced. I got my hand over his mouth and nose, pulled him down, and held him there, kicking, until I felt sure he was dead.'

She flushed, maternally.

'Oh, sir, *really* . . . !'

'And, the whole time, you were on the landing doing the curtain! Now, go and fetch the police in here again!'

He sat looking sourly at the bread and butter.

She exploded into a shy laugh and threw up her hands and went once again:

'Oh, sir, *really* . . . !'

'Really!'

'No, Mr Bowling, you . . .'

'It's true, I tell you! Fetch the police,' he cried angrily.

She cried again:

'Oh, there, how can you, Mr Bowling, really?' and she said that Mr Winthrop had been taken to the morgue, at least, his poor corpse had, and after he, or it, had been cut open, then the police would know a bit more about it. It was thought he'd had a struggle, and his nose and mouth looked bruised, and Miss Brown was checking up all latchkeys, to see if any were lost, and perhaps been picked up by the assassin. She said Mr Winthrop's brother was coming tomorrow, he'd just wired from Skegness, and that his wife was coming today if she could get permission from E.N.S.A. Finally she said that the young detective had confided that he didn't think it was murder at all, and that they often disagreed with the doctors.

'Well, what does he think it is, then?'

'He thinks he had a fit and fell downstairs and banged his poor nose. The blood went to his head, naturally, in that position, and then his heart failed. Nothing was stolen, you see, so far as is known.'

'I see,' said Mr Bowling quietly.

Suddenly he remembered that not a soul had remarked on his scratched hand.

He pulled it out of his pocket, and Alice cried at once:

'Oh, that Moggie, she scratched mine just the very same, and only last night, in the very same place—look!'

He looked and thought:

'Now I *am* going to vomit!'

. . . When the post mortem and inquest brought in an open verdict, and when nothing whatever happened of any kind, his mood grew restless and bitter. He thought: 'It's quite absurd. Chaps do a murder, and then go about in the Hell of a sweat waiting to be arrested: I go about in the Hell of a sweat because I'm afraid I *won't* be arrested!' It had its comical aspect, and sometimes he would stop in the street, pink with sun and health, and burst out laughing. 'I'm blowed!' he'd cry brightly. 'Well, I dunno, I'm sure! Americans think our police too wonderful, what? What am I to do, go into a police station and do in the sergeant there and then? Or what?' He would stand in the park staring about, hands deep in his trousers pockets, and bursting out laughing. 'Struth! What?' He would stare at the kids, and the yachts, and the Palace, and wander round by the artificial garden. Then, in another mood, a very frequent one indeed, he'd wander about Notting Hill Gate and Ladbroke Grove, knocking back one or two in The Mitre, and then wandering up the hill and into St John's Church, kneeling at the altar there and pleading with real tears in his eyes: 'Lord—*why* don't you want me?' He had fits of getting tight for about a week, mid-day and at night, and then not having a drink at all for a fortnight or so. 'Recuperating,' he called it to Queenie when they met sometimes, 'what? Ha, ha! Go without drink for a bit and it gives you a proper kick next time when you start again!' She always said, these days: 'Oh, now, Bill, I nearly forgot, I want you to meet an awfully nice girl I've got for you, I *know* you'll like her!' She made him laugh. He liked them all right, but there was no heart to it.

For some reason or other, he thought, his life-handicap was to be deprived of love, and by love he meant real and mutual love, not pyjamas and a bed. But there, everyone had their handicap, some blokes had to be blind, deaf or lame, or cursed with a mother-in-law of the music hall school, and what could be worse than that? Life clearly wasn't meant to be easy. One woman Queenie trotted out, he liked very much, she had sense, but there you were, she had nothing else at all, except a very large pair of feet, she kept making him think of football. She had these feet, upon which she shoved enormous brogues, they had great brown tongues like desperately thirsty spaniels. Yet she had the nicest ideas and a soothing voice, didn't belch smoke in your face, or cover your lips with orange paint. She said what was the matter with him was that he wasn't go-ahead enough.

'Go-ahead enough,' he pondered reasonably against himself.

'Yes. You don't mind my saying it?'

'Oh, I'm always self-analysing,' he said cheerily.

'Well, for instance, your music. And your unhappy marriage. If . . .'

'Don't tell me,' he interrupted, laughing, 'if I'd got it in me, I'd have made a go of it! You don't need influence, all you need is hard work and the ruddy will to win! Yes, I daresay you're right, my dear!' He sat looking rueful.

'Well, there's something in it, Bill? But I'm not being in the least defeatist, dear, I'm thinking of now, and I'm thinking of the future. You're not old.'

He smiled ruefully.

'I'm afraid I'm a bit of a wash-out,' he said, 'all the same!'

'Oh,' she cried, so sincerely, 'you are so wrong, Bill. There's lots in you. If *only* my love for you could bring it out?'

He smiled wanly.

'You don't love me,' he said, knowing he spoke the truth, 'you only think you do! You want a home, you want a man, you want a background! Everyone does!

*

His move into the brand new flat was a mental effort. At the back of his mind he respected the police, and he did really expect to receive visitors any minute. The police were not fools, and although there were such things as flukes, accidents and mistakes, there wasn't very much you could get away with nowadays. You could fool some of the people some of the time, or even all of the people, but you couldn't fool all of the people all of the time. He didn't really know whether to move in or not, he was fed up with where he was, and with Joan and Alice, and with Mr Gunter who now seemed under the impression a new friendship had been formed between them. Mr Gunter could not take a hint, and Mr Bowling thought, 'If I don't go now, Gunter will be occupying Winthrop's place on the stairs next, and that will be a very dull finish!' He wandered about with his hands in his pockets, listening to every door bell and wondering if it was for him.

He went into Notting Hill Gate and vaguely ordered a piano for the new flat. It cost a packet, and he was in two minds about buying it, saying to the man, 'I really don't know, old lad, I haven't really made up my mind to take it,' and then the next minute, having asked for a record of *Jerusalem*, saying, 'Well, I'd better have the piano as well, I suppose.' He smiled and pulled out his wallet. 'I don't want to disappoint you, I expect you get some commission.'

'It's exceedingly thoughtful of you, sir!'

'Not a bit of it, if we can't think about each other these times, well . . . !'

'Exactly, sir! But I appreciate it all the same!'

'O.K. I'll pay in notes.'

He carted vast sums about with him, it was a sort of complex after all those frightful years of sitting on divans wondering how far he could make 1s 8d go, let's see, ten Gold Flake, a pint of Mild, a packet of notepaper, or else . . .

'Thank you very much, sir. I'll make you out a receipt.'

'Right you are, old lad!'

But he wandered out of the shop and down the hill, forgetting the receipt and his change, which was duly waiting for him when he did in fact move in. The block of flats were called Addison Heights, which wasn't a bad idea, they were nine storeys high, and looked pretty imposing. The moment he went through the swing doors he felt pretty good, as one often did under the influence of the magical word Change. He would have a bit of a binge, ask simply everyone he knew, and tell them all to bring friends, and they'd have a good time, they'd all swim in gin and whisky, providing the shops had any left still. He'd play the piano for them, and he might even croon! His spirits rose. There was a warm, homely smell about Addison Heights, despite the newness and cleanness of everything and everyone, and he hoped he would be able to make his flat have the illusion of homeliness. And if, in the middle of the party, the bell rang and he opened the door and a sinister figure stood there, well, that was part of the drama of the time, and it was what he was playing for, was it not? Are you Mr Bowling? Yes, what can I do for you? This is Scotland Yard, and I have called in connection with the death of Harold Winthrop, at Number Forty.

The party would break up into little, frightened groups.

It would soon be buzzing.

'I say—poor old Bill's been *arrested!*'

'*What*, dear? *Arrested?*'

They'd see him marched off. He'd smile, hiding his handcuffs with his mackintosh.

'It's nothing, some mistake, I expect, don't worry? Have a good time—or I shall worry. Queenie, you'll look after them . . . ?'

He went through the swing doors and half a dozen porters in amber uniforms touched their caps respectfully.

It was so very nice.

CHAPTER IX

ALICE wept what he called Elephant Tears, when he left, seizing him in a starchy embrace in the hall, and vowing she would never look at another man as long as she lived. He told her, well, that wasn't long, was it, not unkindly, but it was so obvious, and he reminded her that she'd had a pretty good innings. 'And don't forget those railings have been removed, Alice,' he wagged a finger at her. 'Don't want to find yourself on your back on the wet grass!' She pouted and sulked, complaining that he hadn't even told her where he was going, or where his letters were to be posted to. 'Not likely!' he said. He gave her a kiss and left.

With Joan it had been much worse, and there had been no kiss. She'd wept too, making him explode with: 'Was ever man so loved as I am!' with an ironical, twisted expression on his face. He got angry with Joan, refusing to tell her where he was going, either, and refusing to promise to visit her at Smith's.

'Now my dear,' he told her, 'I'm not going to tell you I'm coming when I know jolly well I'm not coming!'

'Please come,' she begged.

'I am not coming! And that's that!'

'I think you're a swine!'

'You must think what you like, old thing,' he sighed, and did up his valise.

'At least tell me where you're going, Bill?' she implored.

He said, bored, 'Oh, Guildford, if I must say something.'

'I'll write you G.P.O., Guildford,' she said at once, and when he had gone sat down weeping and writing to him at Guildford. 'Darling Bill, I'm so lonely, please be kind . . .' and the very next morning, after she'd kissed it and posted it, ran slap into him strolling along the High Street there, without a hat and

77

coat. She was furious. 'I thought you said you were going to Guildford, Bill? Of all the mean, lowdown tricks, and of all the mean . . . !'

He bolted up a side street, her after him, and the public looking interested. They chased along and found themselves in Holland Walk. He ran like a hedgehog, and she ran like a hare, and was soon up to him in her red and green hat, saying how they were made for each other, and why couldn't he be decent and give a girl a break.

He felt strangely amused, running like this about London, and leaned up against the fence to get his breath back.

'When the blitz was on,' he commented, panting, 'I was walking up here one night, and a shower of incendiaries dropped all round the bally place. There was a fire on the roof of one place, and I knocked the people up and helped put it out. When I'd finished, the old cow said, thanks so much, do you mind carrying these buckets downstairs before you go, I do dislike them up here. I said, but of course, madam, but mayn't I wash up the dinner things before I go? . . . It was the night before that place was burnt out,' he said, pointing at Holland House.

'Bill, couldn't we be together? A sort of trial? I know I could make you happy.'

'No one can make me happy,' he snapped in sudden anger, and started to stride off.

Perplexed, she stared after him, her sad little voice wailing: 'Oh . . . *Bill* . . . !'

He had a violent reaction against the flat when he got in, and decided it was inhuman and cold. 'It doesn't breathe,' he thought in sudden despair.

He stared about it, wandering up and down the little hall and passage, liking the brown carpet, and liking the velvet curtains, and liking the pictures, such few as were there, Venice, and a boy in brown clothes staring at a blue sky, and at a

Surrealist cat looking as if it didn't know whether to have kittens or go to the pictures. The room with the balcony was nice, the bedroom was nice, the other little room was nice, and the bathroom was nice, and the kitchen was nice and had a nice electric kettle and a long distance view of the roof of the former Earls Court Exhibition.

But it was cold and unfriendly to him and he felt it didn't like him.

When he discovered that it was a cold day for July, and turned the pipes on, he had an idea it was friendlier, even though it thought him a trifle eccentric.

Then he decided that it hadn't got enough of his personality in it yet, and not enough of his things. He played the piano for a bit, jumped up and thought he would do a tremendous shopping expedition. For once, he wished Joan was there, to help him, but to ask her would be fatal.

He went shopping on his own, buying masses of clothes, cigars, drinks, anything that wasn't too severely rationed, and brought the lot home in a taxi. 'I feel like Father Christmas,' he told the porter who helped him in, and felt brighter. But the moment the porter went, the flat was silent and sulky and didn't make a sound of any kind at all. It just threw shadows at him, shadows of himself. 'Oh, my God,' he thought, and stood staring at his parcels. The flat didn't want his parcels. 'What's the good of being Father Christmas,' he thought, 'if there's nobody to give anything to?' He thought: 'I'll go out again, or I shall go nuts!' When the door bell rang, he jumped as if somebody had let off a Tommy-gun. He instantly thought of the police and felt his hands go clammy. He felt glad, in a way. 'Oh, heck,' he whispered to himself, and walked slowly to the front door and opened it. But it was only the porter once again, wanting to know if he needed the daily cleaner, any laundry collected, and would he subscribe to the Red Cross Penny A Week Fund?

'Yes, old boy, rather,' he said to everything, and presently got his hat and tootled along to see old Queenie.

Her husband was out and she was having a bath.

They had a chat through the half open door, Queenie saying not to come in, she wasn't a sight for young eyes any more, and laughing.

'I want to throw a party,' he called through. 'I've got a new flat, old dear, and I want you to be kind of hostess.'

She was delighted.

'A party? What fun! Of course I will! When?'

'Tomorrow night,' he called. Through the crack in the door he saw her soaping her knees. One of her knees had a whitish scar where she had come a cropper off her scooter as a child.

She went in for huge soap tablets and an enormous loofah.

'I suppose you couldn't put me up for tonight, my dear?' he called.

'Tonight?' she called, surprised. 'What's wrong with the flat, then?'

'Oh, I dunno! They're having the drains up,' he improvised, laughing a little and saying candidly, 'no, I'm lonesome tonight!'

'Silly ass,' she said. 'Of course you can stay, dear, if you want to, you know that, Rodney'll be pleased to see you.'

'Where is the old warhorse?'

'He'll be in directly.'

'He doesn't like me, does he?'

'What? He thinks you don't like him!'

The evening was alcoholic but unsensational.

He spent the whole of the next morning with Queenie fixing up with people they knew to come to the party, such as were not in the Forces and so on. 'Better call it a bottle party,' Queenie had decided, 'just in case of shortage.'

He felt better.

When he went back to the flat, he thought it was better pleased with him. A Belgian refugee was waiting to do the cleaning, a round woman in a green overall, who could not speak any English. She was sad and didn't smile, and when he admitted her, just got on with everything as if she had been there all her life. When she saw the chaos of bottles and glasses next morning, her expression didn't change, she just got on with the washing-up.

. . . The party was a success. Nothing happened to make it so, it just was. Nothing happened of any kind. People talked and drank, and for two hours it seemed to be gathering impetus as if to reach some interesting and culminating point, such as a cabaret or stage turn, but nothing happened beyond the glasses being filled again, and then it seemed to have reached high level, where it happily remained, a drone of contented voices, alcoholic giggles, and a density of smoke which could not be released on account of the blackout. They opened the front door and it drifted slowly out there, left and right along the fifth floor corridor. Sometimes some of them went down in the lift to the club in the basement. It was a squash club, and there were three courts with dancing going on in each of them. At the cocktail bar, Mr Farthing was sitting airing his sonorous voice.

Mrs Farthing often told everyone that Mr Farthing ought to be dead, he was far too good for this world. There was a kind of hint that she meant it, but nobody quite knew for certain what her reactions to him were. Poor Mrs Farthing had twisted legs, due to a prenatal fall, and she was obliged to walk as if she was on a very wide horse. Everyone said: 'She is such a dear. It's so sad. And that loathsome man . . .'

Mr and Mrs Farthing were employed by the company which ran Addison Heights, and for a salary they looked after the squash club, the restaurant and a kind of furniture shop full of things to put on mantelpieces, nothing heavy, book-ends and lamp shades and paper knives and so on.

Mrs Farthing spent all day in the restaurant, and when dinner was over (two and threepence, five courses), took the lift down to the basement. Mr Farthing spent all day in the shop which was in the reception hall next to the restaurant, and on all possible occasions hurried down, by lift or stair, to see how Daphne was getting on in the club bar.

Although there was nearly always something very wrong with the world in general, on this particular evening Mr Farthing was in an excellent humour, Daphne having been nice to him, and a reasonable allowance of draught beer in from the brewer's, it was getting a job to get Scotch Ale at all. Mr Farthing's particular grievance, speaking generally, was against an entity which he sneeringly called Capitalists. It was understood all round that Mr Farthing was that very thing in embryo, and which was the very reason for his bitterness. He said in the same sentence what he thought about Capitalism, and what he would do when *he* made his pile, which, as his wife said, and as Euclid said, was absurd. 'You're impossible, Alfred!' she said. 'Do dry up.' He never did dry up, his well was inexhaustible. He sat on that red stool of his, on the clients' side of the bar, looking like an anthropoid ape. He had no forehead and a bald, sloping head, and a great, stupid jowl set in a soured line. His neck was yards thick.

The moment Mr Bowling came into the club that first time, he spotted him. His little eyes appeared to vibrate in unison with his lips, as he labelled him out loud.

'Hallo,' he said behind his hand to Daphne, 'another bloated Capitalist, from the look of it!' Mr Farthing knew all about everyone at Addison Heights. When he felt he didn't know enough about anyone, he stood one of the porters a beer and was thereby enabled to hurry to his wife and say behind his hand: 'Told you so—Capitalist,' and, sometimes: 'I told you so, she's nothing more nor less than a Pro!' A Pro was a thing which Mr Farthing had many times picked up in the top end of the Bayswater Road, and who had done well for herself since. When Mrs Farthing said: 'Oh, dry up for God's sake, she's a nice girl, leave her alone,' he hurried down to Daphne. Putting his hand over his mouth, he said to her: 'We'd better watch Number 167! Very tasty—very sweet!'

When Mr Bowling came in with his friends, Daphne said:

'It's Mr Bowling. He joined the club this afternoon. But he doesn't play squash.'

Daphne was a large square sort of girl, and favoured a skirt which was the replica of a kilt. It was a great asset just before closing time, when men were at their most abandoned, for they would stand her Egg Flips and Advocat in order to be allowed to say: 'Does a Scotsman wear trousers, my dear? I always wanted to know!' At Christmas, under the influence of mistletoe, it was discovered that Daphne wore little brown drawers under her kilt, with embroidery down the outside. It had been a great occasion, only marred by the ferocity of Mr Farthing's countenance, who sat writhing on his red stool in jealousy, unable to prove any proprietary claims. He vowed that men were very coarse, and that he hated a man who didn't know how to hold his drink. When he saw that Mr Bowling was not only a bloated Capitalist, but was tight too, his scorn showed itself quite plainly, notwithstanding he was supposed to be host, and it was up to him to encourage business. He heard Mr Bowling's refined accents, as he ordered expensive things like liqueurs, and he noticed his courteous treatment of Daphne (and her reaction to it, 'Yes, Mr Bowling, we've still got some Kümmel, but I'm afraid it's 1/6 here, sir?'), and he saw him pull out great wads of notes and smile round at everyone except himself. He saw Mr Bowling give him one glance and then turn away again. Mr Farthing's jaw set. He would not forget that little incident. It was the kind of treatment he did *not* put up with, who did he think he was, did he realise who was the host here?

Suddenly Mr Farthing started to talk in a very loud voice about Capitalism, never taking his eyes off Mr Bowling, who had asked for a newspaper.

'I never read the newspapers,' Mr Bowling smiled at Daphne, 'unless I want to see something particular.'

But Daphne hadn't got a paper, she was terribly sorry.

'It's all right. Not important at all.'

'Capitalism,' Mr Farthing bellowed to a few cronies, but never taking his eyes off Mr Bowling, 'has got this country into the mess we're in. And I defy anyone to challenge me.' He stopped. Out of the din of chatter and laughter and dancing and the dance band and the clacking of bottles and glasses, he distinctly heard Mr Bowling laugh and say to his friends:

'Who is that terrible fellow?'

Mr Farthing's anthropoid features flushed a deep vermilion.

CHAPTER X

AT the red painted cocktail bar, Mr Bowling's neighbour was drawing an arc with a small compass, so that it travelled over an imaginary map from a point bang on the Coach and Horses in Notting Hill Gate, right round, arcwise, cutting Kensington High Street, Olympia, Brook Green and Shepherds Bush. Nobody quite knew what he was talking about, at this stage of affairs, but he was a nice chap who had been expelled from Eton. Unless you thought a bit, he didn't look that type, and he was very well dressed and well off. He still wore the tie he was not entitled to, but it was rarely that anything drastic happened, the latest occasion being a few months back, when somebody had walked up and socked him in the middle of Marble Arch. What struck Mr Bowling, in his delightfully fuddled condition, was this arc; he thought: 'Ah, my background! There is a line of pubs on that arc, and I know them all! What a wash-out!' This started a train of thought which was gloomy. It started to make him sober. He had a gin and lime juice, which always made him sober after a binge. He began to get a bit maudlin. His head cleared and he felt tired, and he became aware that something this evening had depressed him without him realising it at the time. A chap called Mr Nandle.

He was elderly and tall and very weak-looking in character, and he'd come in with a few people during the evening, exclaiming, 'Why, I seem to remember you, Mr Bowling, years ago,' and it turned out he had married a woman who had known Mr Bowling's stepmother, back in the days when he had still been at school. And although expressions of delight were inevitable, 'delighted to see you, old man, what'll you have, come right in,' it now struck him that any connections with the past depressed him to a quite unbelievable extent. He was a washout, and what was the good of looking so far back, it only made you wish for that Barrie-esque Second Chance, which could never come. Mr Nandle had gone (wearing clothes like Bernard Shaw), saying: 'I'm going back to Knockholt now, I shall certainly have to tell the wife about this, she'll want you to come and stay a weekend,' but depression lingered and increased. He thought: 'Stay the weekend? I belong to London now. My back is to this shabby arc of noisy pubs. I don't want to think about the country or the past.' He leaned on the counter, wanting to get tight again. Mrs Nandle, he remembered, wore tweedish clothes too, and had an extraordinary woman friend. Old Nandle used to chop wood and things, and come in and be told: 'Did you wipe your boots? I do wish you would, Delius? Lady Wilton is coming to tea.' It was very sordid altogether. Poor Mrs Nandle lived in a kind of No Man's Land. She didn't fit in here, and she wasn't really asked to fit in with Lady Wilton either who, although only the wife of a bank account, thought she was the cat's whiskers. 'Why did I say I'd go down there?' he asked himself. 'In that dreadful little house of theirs?' Yet he felt he would go down there. He felt there was that about the incident of meeting old Nandle again which was significant, for good or evil, in the way that such odd little reunions sometimes were. You lived to say: 'If I hadn't met old So-and-So that night, I'd never have done so-and-so,' and either you were highly pleased or badly deflated.

'Oh, Hell,' he muttered, and Daphne leaned forward and beamed.

"Mm?" she said. She had, he noticed, eyes which were such a light brown that they were almost yellow. She had high cheek-bones and did her hair in brown knots.

Queenie came dashing up with a tall girl whose home was in Singapore. They had in tow two gentlemen who were in rather advanced stages, betrayed by glazed eyes.

'Come and dance,' they all cried at him. 'Jetty's got nobody to dance with, Bill . . . !'

He went and danced with Jetty who was called that on account of the way her behind stuck out. She danced on her toes, and when she danced she wore an over-bright smile, as if she was concentrating. She was in the Fire Service, and said she had been chucked out of a fifth floor window that morning by the boys 'into a blanket, of course, those boys, they just won't leave me alone!'

'Really?' he smiled. He became aware that Mr Farthing was in a shadowy corner, watching him.

'Are you doing a war job? If I'm not being impertinent?'

'Not at the moment.'

'Shall you be called up? I'm not . . . ?'

'Grade Three,' he said a little coldly.

She quickly sensed something which made her say quickly:

'I didn't mean to be impertinent . . . ! These people who send white feathers to people, and give them to men in mufti during their leave, I do think it's cheek, they ought . . . !' She didn't finish sentences. 'Don't you? I mean . . . !'

They danced on the red lines of the squash court. The band was up in the gallery. It played an old one: 'If I should fall in love again, I'd fall in love with you again.' Then it played another old one and a chap crooned into a megaphone: 'Johnny Pedlar . . . !' He asked her to sit out, but she looked hopeful, in the way he was so tired of, so he took Jetty to the money machines. They shoved in sixpences and pulled the handle. A shower of sixpences fell out first time, and he gave them to her. She was fascinated and started to lose the lot, *chug*, the handle went, *chug, chug, chug*. After that they had some Scotch Ale. Mrs Farthing smiled at them. She could hardly see over the counter, because of her deformity. 'Isn't she sweet?' Jetty said. Jetty had no sex-appeal, you just couldn't imagine anything, it would be impossible. She knew all about everyone at the Heights, she lived in a one-room flat herself there. 'First floor.' Mr Farthing hovered away over there by the dart board, watching. 'The Farthings live in the basement,' Jetty said. 'But he spends a lot of his time up in that shop on the entrance level. I don't know what he gets up to in there! Mrs Farthing says *she* never goes in there!' What she was trying to say was that Daphne sometimes went in there.

'Daphne looks too sensible,' he remarked.

'Sometimes it's bread-and-butter,' she said.

'Blackmail?' he said.

'Sort-of.'

'There are plenty of jobs in war-time.'

'Do you think people do wrong things because they *want* to, and for no other reason?' she said.

The remark upset him strangely. He said he didn't, but he thought that he did, really. He excused himself and left her abruptly, passing quickly through a ping pong room and a billiard room, where some of his guests had congregated and were having a good time. He slipped out and made for one of the lifts. He noticed that Mr Farthing was still watching him.

He went up in the lift and returned to his flat. The door was open still and various people were collecting hats and coats.

'I'm bored stiff,' he told himself.

But he entered, smiling brightly. A girl in ambulance clothes was bent double with laughter about what another girl in ambulance clothes was saying about her station officer. 'The airs she gives herself, who does she think she is—the Queen of Sheba?'

A tall, thin gentleman leaned drunkenly up against the wall, holding a cluster of tin helmets and gas masks and waiting.

'We . . . ought to go, Celia,' he managed.

Later he managed:

'Celia . . . we really ought to go?'

When they had all gone, he stood amongst the debris feeling bored to death and completely alone.

He sat sorrowfully and wearily down at the piano, which was littered with empty bottles and dirty glasses, feeling self-pitying and sentimental.

He played a little Schubert and thought:
'I really am a tedious fellow.'

Whenever he went in or out of the Heights, Mr Farthing was somewhere in the shadows or recesses, watching him. Very occasionally they said good morning, in cold voices, over-bright with secret dislike, which was mutual. Though Mr Bowling only noticed Mr Farthing in the same sense that he now and then noticed a greengrocer or a postman, thinking vaguely: 'Don't like that fellow particularly,' then dismissing him from his mind until next time, and then dismissing him once again. He had a faint notion that Mr Farthing resented his Harris tweed, for he looked dusty and dowdy himself, always in dreary black, and his gaze swept Mr Bowling's neat figure with contempt. Sometimes Mr Bowling would sit in the entrance lounge having a bit of think. Farthing would be dusting his little shop window, or the ornamental horses stuck there. Mrs Farthing's voice would come from the restaurant door opposite, going: 'Oh, and Sadie, see if we are entitled to any liver, or offal of some kind, will you? I don't know what we're going to do, I don't want to close down unless we can help it.'

'Yes, madam.'

'And I suppose I daren't mention onions?'

'I'll see if I can get one. Mum might sell you one, if not.'

'Would she? Thank you so much. Then I'll give them rabbit stew again, we'll call it hare-sauté.' Her laugh rang out. 'Ha ha ha! Hare-sauté?'

'Very good, madam. What about a spot of tripe?' But madam was still laughing. She came out and hobbled past Mr Bowling going, 'hare-sauté, ha ha ha!' She didn't so much as glance at Mr Farthing, who was watching slyly through the shop glass, rather like a gorilla in its cage waiting for bananas. Mrs Farthing went along through the little garden affair that had been built, which had neat wooden seats all round it, and which also had dog messes all round it, dogs were a problem in London flats.

Porters wandered to and fro, different faces each week, owing to the call up, they were old men and boys now.

Mr Bowling liked to sit there when autumn grew colder, enjoying the sense of movement, and reading any letter which may have come for him, by the electric fire there.

One autumn morning, he sat and read a letter from Mrs Nandle, which had embossed headings at the top announcing: 'The Rookery, Knockholt.'

Even as he sat and told himself he would not go near the place, he knew that he was going, and presently Mr Farthing was in a position to overhear him telephoning Godfrey Davis's for a drive-yourself car, and enquiring about petrol coupons.

Mr Bowling put back the receiver and thought:

'I don't know why I am going down there for the weekend. I'm used to this place now, I quite like it, it's like home. Well, perhaps it will make me look forward to coming back?'

He thought it was as good a reason as any for going anywhere at all. But when, having got back, he stood staring at his empty flat, he thought:

'Oh, my God, here I am again? Now what?'

And then he thought:

'What *is* the matter with me?'

CHAPTER XI

MR NANDLE was perfectly delighted when he heard that Mr
Bowling had accepted the invitation for a weekend at The
Rookery, chiefly because Mrs Nandle said, in the same tones
that she said, 'Have you wiped your boots, Delius?' that Mr
Bowling would never accept. She said if she knew anything at
all, she knew that Mr Bowling was extremely sophisticated and
led the fast London life. 'He's so go-ahead, Delius,' she said.
'And you're so slow!' After that, she said once again that he
never made friends. She said Mr Bowling would be bored stiff
at The Rookery. 'What on earth shall we do with him?'

She discussed it with her friend whose nickname was Niggs.
Her real name was Miss Souter, she was one of the original
Souters, pronounced Suiter, her family had been concerned in
the relief of Ladysmith, 'Quite a long time ago now, of course,'
Delius Nandle explained to visitors, 'one of her uncles, I believe
it was.' Delius stood by the fire when there were guests, wearing
old-fashioned knickerbockers, and fulsome shooting jackets,
and pullovers which Mrs Nandle knitted for him, they had huge
ribs in them and were usually yellow. He called her Fairy though
there was something weighty and bespectacled and formal about
her. Very occasionally, she put on some blue trousers with
creases down the sides. They had an Airedale with a great,
grinning face, called Pots.

Pots always knew when visitors were expected, and he grinned
even more, because he was the medium whereby the family got
over their shyness, bending all the time to feed him and pet him,
and say what a good ratter he was. When the weather, as a topic,
had faded out, there was always Pots, and Delius was quite in
order to stoop and say—'Rats?' in the middle of tea, and it was
quite in order for Pots to let out a bloodcurdling scream, and

dive like a bear at the terrified visitor's feet. Things then went with a swing, Fairy saying apologetically, 'Oh, Delius, how naughty of you,' and Miss Souter crying: 'Oh, that naughty dog, but he is such a wonderful ratter!' The visitor, snatched from the very arena wherein the Martyrs of Old endured similar agonised moments, got out a twisted smile of joy, mentally resolving never to come to The Rookery again.

This morning, Pots was in excellent form, he enjoyed the autumn, not minding country mud at all, or deluging rain, and was proud to be in a position to assist the problem of entertaining a guest for the weekend, by the presentation of a rat he had caught in the scullery last week. He brought it in, both of them grinning, and one of them with a tail wagging ferociously, and deposited it at the foot of Mr Bowling's bed, where, appalled beyond measure, little Miss Souter trod on it and let out a catcall which could have been heard in Tonbridge. Fairy came dashing up the oak staircase, bumping her head on the low rafter there, and getting ready to cry: 'I *told* him to wipe his boots, Niggs, men really are the limit—and after all that Ronuk!' But it was much worse than that.

'Rats,' cried Niggs hysterically, and very rashly, for Pots gave one wild leap and seized her uproariously by her fat ankles.

Delius came in ready to say:

'I don't see any car coming up the road yet, my dear? You did say he was driving down, didn't you?'

Fairy Nandle said, never mind what she did say, just listen to what she had to say now, take that dog outside to start with, and lock him up in the shed until Monday and then come back and pick a rat up from the guest room.

'I sometimes wish we had never bought a dog,' she said angrily, and looking like a witch, 'and I wouldn't have, had I known you couldn't control it, Delius! You really are the most helpless man! And just look at your boots, have you wiped them?'

Delius got petulant when cornered, and was apt to be snappy.

His crab-coloured face took on a resentful demeanour, and he complained that he was treated without proper respect, and like a child in his own house. 'Am I master in my own house, or am I not?' he snapped, knowing full well the answer, and always getting it.

'No, you're not! I don't know why I agreed to marrying you, I didn't in the least want to! I'm perfectly happy here with Niggs . . . Take the dog out. And then come back for the rat. And then go and scrape your boots.'

Sulking, Delius seized Pots by the collar and dragged him out to where the car was kept under sheets, 'until after the war, you know, it's our war effort, self-denial, Niggs thought of it,' and then he returned with a shovel.

After that, Niggs and Fairy set to again with brooms and Ronuk, telling him he couldn't come back until eleven, 'for your Ovaltine. And must you keep pacing up and down? Mr Bowling can't possibly get here until twelve.'

Delius went and sat in the shed with Pots, thinking about things, and wishing, as always, nobody was coming for the weekend. It was always like this. The two women would make him feel small, and he would make stupendous efforts to look big. Then he would be allowed about two sherries, which would make him talk too much. And there would be Hell to pay afterwards. He had only gone to Bowling's flat because of meeting a man in the city he knew called Minson, who happened to know somebody else, who happened to know somebody else, who was going to the party. Delius saw it was a chance for a blind-up, and as Fairy was away just then he thought he'd risk it. Now he realised he must drop a hint to Bowling not to say how tight he got that night, or how tight everyone else got, either. He sat listening to the rain teeming down, and pricked his large red ears for the sound of a car. It came at about noon, and sure enough there was Bowling, driving an Austin 12. He saw Delius coming out of the shed, and he waved. He had enjoyed the drive down, rain and all, and had stopped several times for a wet, and felt pretty good. The moment he saw Delius and their flat little mushroom house, he wanted to turn round and drive for his life. But it was too late now.

Through the window, Fairy and Niggs saw the car in the rain. They at once rang the bell for the daily to stand by, rather like a stage manager signalling the warning for house lights, curtain going up, and gave quick little glances around to see that everything was genteel. They were both anxious to create a good impression, Mr Bowling lived such a hectic life, and was obviously monied. Lady Wilton had been telephoned for, to lend tone at teatime, notwithstanding she hadn't a single original thought in her stupid head, and notwithstanding one of her brothers was in a mental home for inebriates.

'I do hope she can come,' Mrs Nandle feared, and went to telephone anybody else 'suitable' she could think of. 'The Wilsons? Oh, *no*, with that stutter of hers, and all that disgusting chatter about babies' diseases.'

'What about Mrs Elton?' Miss Souter rather wondered. 'She was very interested in Ladysmith and seems well read.'

'Well . . .'

'Or the Mathews, dear? Her brother is at the Treasury.'

The two ladies thought Mr Bowling's entrance perfectly charming. They had rather forgotten him after all these years, it would have been dreadful if it turned out he wasn't a gentleman, Delius was so feeble with men, no wonder he hadn't a single friend. There followed introductions, mentioning Ladysmith, though rather a long time ago now, of course, and mentioning rain, and leading up to rats, but sideskirting to sherry and cocktails, whereby Mr Nandle was in order to stand by the log fire and puff out his chest and say portentously:

'Well, h'ar—and how has the world been treating you?'

It wasn't that Mr Bowling thought unkindly against the Nandles, or against Miss Souter; how, indeed, could he think unkindly against people who, according to their inherited ideas, and according to their lights, were doing their best to entertain him? It was just that he was good-humouredly fond of analysis, not only of himself, which was introspective and apt to be monotonous, and he liked to sit back and consider everyone. It might be that he despised the other person, but he was not unconscious of the fact that they were fully entitled, and welcome, to judge and despise him.

And when it came to him that he was going to murder poor old Delius Nandle, he did not think, well, now, this is a shoddy return for a delightful weekend! He thought, instead, upon matters to do with Destiny, wondering, for instance, whether up in God's Kingdom, there had long ago been placed a little flag, marking in very neat print: 'This is the time and the hour for a poor old chap called Delius Nandle: he will be killed, for no particular *worldly* reason—but for *my* reason.' He said and thought very sadly: 'I didn't want to come here. I didn't ask him to my party. I didn't want to be reminded of my past. And I am not really having a nice weekend at all, it's Hellish, with the rain teeming down the entire time, drenching that depressing stone stork out there in the front garden. I could easily think up some excuse and drive back to town—but I'm not going to. I know it perfectly well.' He also thought instantly: 'This time next week, without any doubt whatever, I shall be in prison.'

Under which circumstances wasn't it common sense to enjoy a bit of country?

He stared through the window at the stork, feeling sorry it had been on the dole for so long—there were no indications that the Nandles had had any children.

While he sat day-dreaming, Mrs Nandle said various things which captured his attention and made him feel inwardly angry. She said things which she ought not to have said, the more so if they were true. Perhaps they were and perhaps they weren't. That was not the point.

Niggs was out in a yellow mackintosh, with Delius, feeding the chickens. There had been real eggs for tea, and Pots had been allowed in, and all the stories about him had been told, including the one about the rat up in the guest room.

And now Fairy Nandle, bent at some knitting, 'a jumper for Delius, next Christmas, Mr Bowling,' assumed a confidential tone, and by long and devious routes got the conversation round to delicate matters. She was adroit, and was quickly able to say to a comparative stranger:

'Poor Delius, I'm afraid you find him very dull and weak! He gets simply hopeless when he has had a glass of sherry. But you must be tolerant, and I feel you are. I do believe we all ought to be tolerant, and I'm sure you do. I could have divorced him, you know,' she got out suddenly. 'Several times.'

A feeling of dislike fell like drops of poison into his blood, and began to circulate.

You see, he said to himself, I just cannot kill women. I'm sorry, Delius.

But after all, why should the old chap complain?

He wouldn't know anything?

Mrs Nandle bent over her knitting, wearing huge horn-rimmed glasses, and her glamorous blue trousers. She was sixty if she was a day.

She said she felt Mr Bowling was a man one could talk to, and she didn't know why she was telling him all this, but Delius had been dreadful several times, 'with little blondes.' He thought: 'I don't wonder! And you are telling me this simply because you tell everyone this!'

When the shadows fell, the two women fell about the place arranging the blackout. Delius said all about how they always kept the stirrup pump in the corner of the porch, and they always kept the bath full of cold water. He said he had fire-watching to do, but would not wake anybody up when he came in.

Mr Bowling was shown upstairs to a little green and white room, with curtains and wallpaper dotted with scenes from *Peter Pan*. Mr Nandle started to say, 'Once, we rather hoped

. . . that is to say . . . however!' and broke off lamely. 'Fond of children?' he enquired, blushing.

'Very,' said Mr Bowling.

'Well, there it is . . . !'

'It's stopped raining,' Mr Bowling said, wondering what time to murder his host. Perhaps tomorrow morning. Or tomorrow evening, just before leaving. In that shed. Oh, some idea would turn up.

'Well, goodnight, Bowling!'

'Goodnight, old chap!'

'Hope you'll be comfortable? I think Fairy's put a hot water bottle . . . and there'll be early morning tea, and . . .'

'Marvellous! It's so nice of you to have asked me down.'

'We're delighted to have you. We're very lonely people, you know. But of course you don't know the meaning of the word! You gay Londoners! H'm. Well, goodnight?'

They shook hands.

Mr Nandle was thinking: 'Charming chap. Hope he isn't bored.'

And Mr Bowling was thinking:

'The old boy's nostrils may give me a bit of trouble. Peculiar shape. But apart from that, I shouldn't think the poor old chap had a kick in him.'

He went to bed.

That night, Miss Souter, who had shared the double bedroom with Mrs Nandle for years, woke up in fright and declared she had dreamt that a funeral cortège had approached The Rookery. She said it was quite real. Both women discussed this. They both wore turbans on their heads, and had plastered their faces with grease. Upstairs, Delius was thumping about in his lonely room, and they looked at their watches hanging on the bedrail and saw that it was as late as two in the morning. 'What is the matter with him?' Fairy said crossly, and got out of bed and opened the door. 'Delius?' she called in a hissing voice, for fear of waking Mr Bowling.

His door opened.

'Hallo . . . ?'

'What on earth are you doing?'

'Doing?'

'It's two o'clock, Delius . . .'

'I was reading Trollope, *Barchester* . . .'

'Do go to sleep. Niggs is having dreadful dreams,' Mrs Nandle complained.

The grandfather clock complained downstairs, and she went back and her door shut.

'There's something very uncanny in the place,' Miss Souter said in the darkness.

Out in the shed, Pots started up a tremendous barking.

'I dreamt of a funeral cortège, and I dreamt it was Mr Bowling in the coffin,' Miss Souter said, 'yet I'm sure he was *alive*.'

'I never think of death,' Mrs Nandle remarked. 'I suppose one ought to more often.'

'I suppose we all ought to.'

'Life seems such a permanent affair.'

'I do wish people didn't think we were lesbians, Fairy? I know we're the talk of the place.'

'Does it really matter what people think?'

'I often think it does,' Miss Souter said.

'It's Delius's fault. He will talk when he's in his cups, and I expect he tells everyone I'm cold, and not a good wife. But after all, I'm not a chicken, I've told him time and time again that he's had the best years of my life—and what have I had?'

'I'm afraid he's a very stupid man, poor Delius, dear.'

'Yes! I'm very much afraid he is!'

They talked a bit longer about how Mrs Nandle had so nearly been a Mrs Hawk-Smith, and gone to Hong Kong to live, and about how old Delius had popped up, looking helpless, and she'd gone to him as she would have gone to an old dog which has been bumped into by a passing car and left a bit dazed.

But she said she had no idea how stupid he was, really funda-mentally stupid and dull. He said nothing, thought nothing and did nothing. It was sad, but you had to face it. Miss Souter said, well, dear, we were all full of faults, and anyhow Fairy still had her, not that that was saying much, but there was something to be said for ordinary friendship. She said she had never loved a man, and could honestly say she hadn't ever wanted to. 'So I'm lucky,' she said she thought.

Next morning at breakfast, Delius revealed himself to be stupid as ever, he had left the lantern burning all night, the one they kept in the scullery, it both gave a light and saved the pipes from freezing, a new gadget it was. But he had left it on when the weather was quite moderate, and he knew perfectly well that dish cloths and things hung there, and might easily brush against the naked flame. Another thing he had done was to leave the back-door unlocked, so that burglars could just stroll in any old time and help themselves.

'Really, Delius!' the two women thought.

Red and embarrassed before Bowling, he tried to laugh it off with:

'Really, nobody would think I was master here, I don't know what Bowling thinks, I seem to be treated like a schoolboy!'

The following pause was rather pointed, but breakfast conversation seemed to go more brightly after that, despite porridge, and then got almost gay, Niggs saying that she thought Delius was the type who should have grown a beard. What she meant was that a beard would give the illusion that he had a chin, but what she actually said to give point, and to hide Fairy's, 'Beard? Delius? Gracious!' was, 'Beards give such personality, I always think. What do you think, Mr Bowling?' Mr Bowling whose mind was elsewhere, said it depended what one had 'learnt' about such things.

'Learnt?' enquired Niggs keenly. She had been watching a thrush through the window, having swigs at the birdbath.

Fairy and Delius cracked bits of toast with oddly similar pink

and sinewy fingers, and smiled encouragingly at their guest.
There was a nob of porridge on Delius's mauve pullover. It slid
down, interestingly, into the front of his brown trousers.

Mr Bowling, with a bit of a laugh, said that most people had
learnt that the man with a beard was frightfully highbrow and
difficult to know or like, he might even be a professional artist,
and too difficult even to talk to.

Niggs, uncertain whether the accent was on comedy or
drama, said, 'Yes, I *see*,' and started an obscure account of what
a good idea it would be if only somebody would think of driving
a tunnel all the way from here to Germany, and opened up a
Second Front? 'After all,' she said, 'we do such wonderful things,
does it seem so fantastic?' The idea was not pursued, however,
owing to Delius saying, still more obscurely, what about the
man who wears green shirts, then, and laughing for an inordi-
nate length of time. Everyone stared at him until he stopped,
coughing affectedly, and Mr Bowling observed conversationally:
'And the chap who wears red ties is, of course, insane! That is
to say, he is the man of tomorrow!'

After breakfast, he heard Niggs saying to Fairy up on the
landing:

'Mr Bowling's so subtle and go ahead! It's wonderful!'

'Subtle is the word,' Fairy agreed. 'It's a real stimulant. Mental
stimulant. If *only* Delius was like that!'

Then she called to Delius, who was another floor up, and
made one or two enquiries.

'We don't want you to be petulant the entire day,' she called
to him sharply.

Mr Bowling found himself fingering a copy of Kingsley's
Westward Ho!, reading the opening which said: 'The hollow
oak our palace is, Our heritage—the sea,' and reading the flyleaf,
which said in schoolboy script:

'This belongs to D. Nandle, Lower Fifth, Christmas, and
whoever pinches it is a filthy hound. Signed D.N.'

*

The two women had decided to go to church in the evening, and so as it was dry Mr Bowling offered to take them all a drive until then, or at any rate for as long as the petrol lasted. They were delighted, and said there was petrol in the garage.

So they drove to Ashdown Forest, lunched near there, and had a good blow. It made a change. The two women sat in the back, and Delius sat in the front, red-looking and pleased, and having no notion whatever, or intuition, that he was having his last day on earth. He said he thought that but for Russia, we would have been in a fine old pickle by now, and he said he wished he was young enough to have a smack at the Japs. At the back, they said they wondered what it must be like to be Prime Minister at such a time, and what a responsibility it was. And they said they had a picture of Mr Churchill at home, bricklaying because his country thought there was nothing more useful he could do; and they said they had another one of Lady Baldwin making a speech, they thought in Dulwich. Tanks clattered past them, and Mrs Nandle remembered during the last war when you couldn't drive far without soldiers stopping you with fixed bayonets and making you take the seats up. Miss Souter thought English soldiers were more refined nowadays. No sooner had she spoken than a posse of soldiers in German grey stopped the car and told her to get out and look slippy. Appalled, she was so frightened that the Germans had arrived at long last, she scurried out and clutched Mrs Nandle in terror. The Gestapo were here! But they had a great laugh at lunch, because it was only a rehearsal, and a very effective one! We weren't exactly asleep, Mr Bowling laughed and said!

They reached home as it was getting dark, and after a late tea the two ladies took their leave of Mr Bowling, who said he would be gone before they returned.

They said it had been the pleasantest weekend for many a day.

'I'm terribly glad,' Mr Bowling smiled and said.

'I do hope you haven't been bored?'

'I've loved every moment of it . . . !'

'How nice of you, you must come again? Delius is so lonely, even though he has his firewatching.'

Their footsteps went pattering down the path.

Mr Bowling came slowly back to the living room and stood by the log fire. He stared into it, hearing Delius closing the front door and calling: 'Very well, my dear! Yes, my dear . . . !'

CHAPTER XII

Mr Bowling idly kicked the log and watched the sparks fly. The red firelight lit the crease in his trousers, there was something about neatly creased flannel. He thought sadly: 'I'm not going to flatter myself that I am the chosen instrument of Delius's entry into the Next World. It isn't that . . . But what I mean to say is, he doesn't know what's coming, he knows no fear, it won't take long, and surely the point is we should all be prepared to die at any moment of any day, the war must at least have taught us that? The blitz must have taught us that? I mean,' he thought, 'it is up to each of us, isn't it?' And he turned and thought:

'It's a bit different with me—I happen to *want* to go.'

The old dog was barking out there, and Delius said what about letting the brute in for a bit. He laughed sheepishly. 'My wife doesn't allow it, but Pots and I have our secrets!'

The only regret, Mr Bowling thought, was separating the old chap from his dog.

'Do you mind very much if we don't have him in?' he said quietly to Nandle.

Nandle stopped by the door and looked his astonishment. His tall, stooping figure threw an enormous shadow across the low ceiling and across the far wall, blotting out the white alcove there. His face took on a shy, babyish expression, rather quaint, as if he was thinking, oh, dear, I hope my guest isn't going to be hard to entertain, have I said the wrong thing?

'I'm frightfully sorry,' he said to his guest slowly and shyly, and hovering with a hand on the door. 'I thought you liked dogs!'

Bowling was standing with his hands in his pockets.

'I do like them, old chap,' he replied in a breezy way, staring down at his shoes.

'I wouldn't have . . .'

'No, no, I just have a slight headache, as a matter of fact.'

'I say, I'm most . . . !'

'Nothing at all, only a very slight one. I thought the dear old dog, though I love him . . .'

'But of course, we don't want the brute bounding about if you're like that! Look here, I've got some aspirin somewhere!'

'No . . .'

'They're in Fairy's room. I'll go up, it won't take a second.'

'I don't want to trouble you, old man, really.'

'I insist! No, really, it's no trouble at all, Bowling. The reverse.' He went out and there was the sound of his footsteps going up the creaky stairs, all mountainous shadows, and the glimpse of his red, worried face, as if he was thinking: 'I wonder why he said that about Pots, he was so kind to the dog after lunch, had the brute on his knee, even. I hope he's not ill . . . ? I wonder how long he is going to stay, he said he'd be off before Fairy and Niggs got back, but he doesn't seem to be making a move, is he bored?' The lines deepened into his bit of a forehead.

He went up the stairs and went into Fairy's room and hunted about for the aspirin. Coming out, he thought of the cupboard where all the games were put, and he decided that Bowling might care for a game of draughts. He opened the little white cupboard and put in his long fingers. It was rather a dull idea, one supposed, but it might encourage Bowling to go, as a matter of fact he wasn't *frightfully* easy to entertain, he was probably shy, most people were shy in some secret way or other. He felt very shy, as a matter of fact, though it seemed ridiculous, being left alone with Bowling. Perhaps it would be best to leave the draughtboard, after all, and just go down with the aspirin and suggest a drink?

He hesitated, finally deciding to take the board, and suggest a drink as well. And a cigar.

In the cupboard was the Mah Jong set he had given Fairy all those years ago, when he had started the life of an architect's clerk, which he still was. He sighed, thinking of all those years ago, and how wasted they seemed. Wasted? Well, well, who could say if life's minutes and hours and days were ever wasted—until you could judge the thing as a whole? And when, indeed, could you judge it as a whole? Not ever, on this side of the Styx. There was a modicum of beauty and comfort in that, wasn't there?

He closed the cupboard and started to go down the stairs again, the draughtboard in one hand, the aspirin in the other.

Coming round the bend in the creaky stairs, he was astonished to find that Mr Bowling had put out the light. There was just the firelight, its warm, flickering shadows.

'Are you there, Bowling?' he began in surprise. He couldn't see him. Was he sitting down, or had he gone out? 'I wonder if you would like a whisky and soda with your aspirin? And then, if you were to sit quietly, before leaving, if you really intend going back tonight though I wish you wouldn't, you know, we might have a game of draughts? I can't remember when I last . . .'

When his voice stopped so suddenly, there was a very remarkable stillness indeed, broken only distantly, in the country kind of way; the old dog wailing out there in his shed; a distant train. The nearer and more vital and intimate sound of the crackling flames in the grate there, eating the green, juicy wood.

And the small sound of the aspirin bottle falling to the parquet; and the slightly bigger sound of the draughtboard falling there too.

And then a sliding, muffled sound, which might have been anything.

And, at last, the closing of a door, two doors; quietly.

. . . Mr Bowling enjoyed that sense of excitement which the Londoner always gets when he has been away for a little time, but is now coming home again. He drove like the wind, leaving the quiet behind him. At Bromley he stopped at an hotel and went in to the noise and the lights. It was gay . . .

In his pocket was Mrs Nandle's little parcel. She had asked

him at lunch-time if he lived anywhere near Brook Green, and when he said he did, she asked him if he would be so very good as to take the little parcel to an address for her, it was fragile and might break in the post. It was a present for someone. He hadn't listened at all closely, merely registering that he would be delighted to deliver the parcel safely. The address was on it in Mrs Nandle's large script.

He forgot it again.

When he reached London he was well-lit and in a bright humour. He felt pleased to see his flat again, the atmosphere was friendly and warm. He mixed a stiff whisky and soda, tossed it back and went down to the club, where, off-handedly, he asked Daphne for a newspaper.

'A newspaper?' she cried cheerily. 'Why, Mr Bowling, it's Sunday!'

He made a grimace.

'How stupid of me! I clean forgot.'

CHAPTER XIII

SUNDAY at the Heights was little different to other days; the club merely opened an hour later, while Mrs Farthing merely put on her green flowing dress with the pink coral beads. Mr Farthing looked just the same, in the same ash-strewn dark suit, sitting on the same stool, looking sullen and vicious and going behind his hand: 'Here he is again—h'mf! And don't think I've forgotten!' when Mr Bowling came in. He heard Mr Bowling ask for a paper and thought he meant the Sunday morning papers, which were on the table to his hand, but he thought: 'I'm not going to pass them to him, B. . . . . Capitalist, let him send one of the servants for them! I suppose he wants to look at his B. . . . . horoscope!' Nearly everybody in the club went by the Sunday horoscopes, even though all vowed how stupid it was and how wrong all forecasts were. A thin, old, redhaired lady with a scar right across her lips, who had made a long profession out of love, but had now succeeded to well earned retirement at the Heights, on the other hand swore by Mr Naylor in the *Sunday Express*, indicating that he had saved her from mistakes time and again. But Captain Batcher, the squash champion rubbed his sweating body down under the shower downstairs and frequently admitted: 'I'm a complete baby with this affair of the stars, old cock,' to his crony Admiral Leopard. 'I swear by Adrienne Arden. *News of the World*, y'know.' Admiral Leopard knew the *News of the World*, he thought it was a paper full of sparkle, but he didn't follow her, 'only alcohol and billiards, what?' The Admiral had a beetroot-coloured face and was very popular because one night he had been exceptionally merry and had mistaken Mr Farthing's little club-office for the gents, the two places being side by side, and Mr Farthing had gone to his desk startled to observe: 'a leak from somewhere—

struth, Daphne, come here quick . . . ?' There was no dancing
on Sundays, Ted Tickler and His Boys having an engagement
at the Locarno Dance Hall, Tooting Bec, where they dealt out
swing and boogy woogy to entranced couples who later repaired
to the Common to stretch their young and aching limbs. Mr
Bowling had a drink with three people with whom he was on
nodding acquaintance, Flight Lieutenant Hollowshaw, the lady
people said wasn't really Mrs Hollowshaw, and the dull girl
people said was really Miss Hollowshaw. The Flight Lieutenant
looked like an eagle, and was suitably reticent about things
everyone wanted to know, and would only let drop tantalising
hints about what Bomber Command really had been up to, and
how Churchill really crossed the Atlantic, and what we really
had done to Berlin since war began. Miss Hollowshaw was
rather like a mouse who had learned to stand on two little legs,
and she said she thought it was a marvellous idea of the Russians
to drop dead bodies of Germans into Berlin streets. Mrs
Hollowshaw had a kind face, and always showed her ring,
because she knew nobody thought she was really married to
Jock. She didn't like talking about dead bodies or war matters,
and lived from hour to hour, never knowing when she would
see Jock again, if ever at all. She liked to talk about the flats,
telling Mr Bowling that the one-room flats here were 'very natty',
and that the two-roomed ones were 'awfully natty, they really
are', and that she thought the three-roomed ones were 'marvel-
lously natty'. She showed oddly long teeth when she smiled,
and he thought she had the thinnest shoulders he had ever
seen. He listened to it all in a dream and had the feeling that
this modern way of living was a very clever invention, when
one thought of the past with its bare and lonely rooms, without
radio or light, and without getting to know anyone in the house,
except the forward or the boring or the desperate who came
to the door and timidly asked for a shilling for the gas, they'd
run out of change, you'd get it back when they'd been to the
bank—which of course you never did, the poor devils had never

seen a bank, except from the outside. Mr Bowling felt slightly benevolent, as did the Flight Lieutenant, both of them thinking: 'Well, it's all very jolly and gay, but in a day or two, well, who knows?' Daphne was signalled for, and she came smiling along to say in her Sunday manner: 'Same again, sir? I'm afraid we've run out of Scotch Ale, would you like some bottled lager?'

'What about some rum?' suggested Hollowshaw all round.

'Rum,' they agreed. 'Good idea . . . !'

'Three large rums, Daph?'

'Not for Phyllis,' Mrs Hollowshaw said quickly. 'You'll make the child tight.'

'Oh, Stee,' Phyllis said to her mother, if it was her mother. 'The way you fuss me!'

Everybody laughed benevolently. Then they cruised over to the machines, searching for sixpenny pieces, Mrs Hollowshaw saying they were so natty, and she adored them, and then they cruised on to the balcony to watch a squash match. Two fat gentlemen in white vests and pants were slamming the ball over the line, darting here and there to catch it on the rebound, plunging forward again to cry: 'Sorry, sir,' and the ball whizzing to and fro at incredible speed making a soft, stinging sound like: *flap, flap.*

'Sorry, sir . . . !'

'Flap!'

'Splendid, good man . . . !'

'Flap . . . !'

And cheers from the gallery.

'It's *awfully* natty,' Mrs Hollowshaw said, leaning on the rail. 'I love to watch it! D'you remember when we went to Bermuda, Phyll? That man who made us laugh so . . . !'

'Sh, Stee, you mustn't talk, dear!'

'Sorry,' Stee whispered, hunching her thin shoulders shyly. 'My mistake, I'm sure!'

Everyone grinned politely in an understanding sort of way. Flight Lieutenant Hollowshaw stared ferociously at the ball as if he had it in mind to dive bomb the bally thing, no target was too small for him, by jove, it was nice to see a bit of movement again, he was getting properly browned off with this leave, it suddenly seemed endless.

Mr Bowling slipped quietly away, smiling benevolently. He became aware, once again, that Mr Farthing was leaning up against his office wall, watching him.

Places, thought Mr Bowling, like tedious people, never seemed so pleasant as when we were about to leave them.

His flat had never seemed so lived-in as it did that night, sitting alone in his sitting room, staring at the two-bar electric fire, which roasted his slippered feet. 'It will be a little cheerless at the police station,' he reflected, and very much regretted the weeks which inevitably had to pass before they got on with the wretched business of dispatching him.

The room was filled with Mozart.

A bit of wind had started up outside, and he could hear leaves being blown about on his stone balcony there, beyond the velvet curtains. How had they got there? The leaves made him think of the country, and the country made him think of their drive on Ashdown Forest, and that made him think of poor old Delius. Poor? Why was he poor? Nonsense, he was not poor at all; he shared with a billion braves the glory of that last, tiny secret which defeated us all. Defeated us? It did nothing of the kind. The sensible and the sincere knew all they needed to know about it? He thought of ghosts which he believed were only the guilty dead, or the innocent-but-worried dead, they were anxious about someone or something. But no ghosts had come to visit him: Ivy, Mr Watson, Mr Winthrop, Mr Nandle. None at all. They were far too busy and happy, and far too intelligent, one would hope, to waste any more time messing about here, a draughty, unsatisfactory place, oh, all right in the summer, to be sure, but, on balance, what did it amount to, you were either too hot or too bally cold, too dry or too wet, too full or too empty, too miserable or too happy! He let out a little laugh. 'B'rf,' his little laugh went. 'I dunno, I'm sure—what? B'rf!' And he stared at his toasting feet. So he sat for a while, ruminating. Presently he figured out: 'They'll get back from church about seven-thirty, they'll telephone for the doctor, who will arrive about eight, say. Then they'll telephone for the police, which will bring it to nine, say. Then they'll say, after a certain type of conversation, Mr Bowling lives at Number 502 Addison Heights, London, W11, we haven't his telephone number, unless poor Delius has it somewhere, do you know if he has, Niggs, my dear?' But the police would say: 'Never mind about that, madam, we can soon ask the operator.' Which would bring the time up to about nine-thirty at the outside, including the instructions from Knockholt Police Station: 'Pick up this chap Bowling—if you can find him—we want to talk to him.' Which would bring the time, roughly, up to, say, nine-forty-five.

He looked at his wristwatch. It was nine-forty-four.

'H'm,' he thought, and felt pleased to have had a little Mozart while there was time.

He got up and stretched himself, then went into the bedroom and switched on the light. Where other people would have started to undress sleepily, yawning in a pleased fashion, or in a displeased fashion because they were thinking, Hell, that ruddy Ambulance Station again tomorrow, and all those pitiful L.C.C. lecturers babbling about broken spines, Mr Bowling started packing a small suitcase. He put in a spare shirt, pyjamas, socks, handkerchiefs and dressing gown, remembered collars and shaving kit in the bathroom, and closed the case quietly and put it on the little oak table in the little hall, ready. He looked at his watch and strolled back to the sitting room. He lit a cigar and paced dreamily up and down. Every now and again he looked at his watch, and the minute hand crept round towards ten.

He had a sudden worry, which had occurred to him before.

'I shall be pretty well sold,' he thought ruefully, 'if they bring in a verdict of Unsound Mind. D'you realise, old man, what it'd mean?. . . It'd mean that bally asylum place, with Ronald True and that crowd—for the rest of my days!'

It worried him. No motive, you see, he thought over and over again. Though, I suppose I could invent a quarrel—but don't you see that will spoil my idea? I'm sure I don't appear mad, and I'm jolly well not mad, surely plenty of people would testify to that, Queenie . . . Queenie? No, the old pet might pop into the witness box and say he *was* mad, with the idea of saving his neck. It was a bit of a spot. He thought: 'Hell! H'm.'

He would just have to risk it, that's all.

It would have to be a sporting chance, all in with the rest.

He glanced again at his watch. It had just gone ten.

When it turned eleven, he began to feel very irritable. He was still pacing about, suitcase ready, hat and coat ready.

At midnight, he put on the radio again, hearing Big Ben and the midnight news.

He turned it off again in anger, and wandered about the place until one. He thought:

'If I go to bed, they'll damn well turn up and I shall have to dress again.'

His mood grew black.

. . . When dawn came, he was asleep in the armchair, his feet once again by the electric fire.

He slept like a log until eight.

The Belgian refugee had her own key, and she let herself in as usual and proceeded to get Mr Bowling's breakfast. She betrayed no surprise at all when she saw him asleep in the sitting room. She merely went about her duties, not waking him until breakfast was ready, when she drew the curtains and opened a window or two to let out the fug. It was a winterish but beautiful day, there had been a sharp frost, but the sun was busy melting it. Mr Bowling had been dreaming that he was in a cell and the bed was narrow and short and hard.

He shot bolt upright.

'By jove,' he exclaimed. 'Where am I? What?'

The woman said nothing whatever, just putting the chair, so to speak, for him to start his breakfast. Expressionless, she went out and closed the door.

CHAPTER XIV

AT about the same time, Mr Farthing opened the door of his shop. The first thing he always did on a Monday morning, was to switch on the lights, and start doing a spot of sweeping and dusting. There were no windows in the shop, except the front show window looking on to the foyer of the Heights, and the restaurant windows. He was dusting his china horses when he saw Mr Bowling come down in the lift and go out without a hat and coat. He thought he was looking preoccupied. In about two minutes, Mr Bowling returned carrying goodness only knew how many newspapers. He saw him sit on the settee and begin to go through them all carefully. 'Must be very interested in the war,' commented Mr Farthing sourly to himself. 'I wonder what he does. Some safe and cushy job in one of the ministries, little doubt, thirty odd quid a week coming in for doing Sweet Fanny Adams.' When Mr Bowling was again to be seen buying early editions of the evening papers, and to be sitting reading them quickly but carefully, as if afraid of missing something, Mr Farthing thought: 'But of course—racing!' Then he suddenly realised that there was no racing anywhere until next month, he knew that, he could have told him that?

Upon which, Mr Farthing's curiosity knew no bounds.

He thought, scrubbing at his shop front:

'I'd give a quid to know what the devil he does do,' telling himself sourly that he was not in the least curious, he merely felt it was up to all of us to watch people these days, they were very likely spies or Fifth Columnists. 'I notice he doesn't wear a ruddy uniform,' he thought, forgetting that he didn't, either. 'Trust your B. . . . . . Capitalist for that!'

He scrubbed at his windows with a bitter expression. All

114

day he thought about Mr Bowling, telling himself that he had
never for a second forgotten Mr Bowling's remark about him
that first evening in the club, when he'd overheard him ask:
'Who is that terrible fellow?' Mr Bowling need not imagine he
forgot a thing like that; he hadn't and he never would. 'Take it
from me,' he told his wife.

'Dry up,' Mrs Farthing said, bored. 'You're always letting off
wind!'

In the late afternoon, he again saw Mr Bowling go out, and
he saw him come back with copies of the *Evening Standard,*
the *Evening News* and the *Star.* He sat looking up and down
this page and that, throwing a paper aside in a kind of anger,
and taking up another. Afterwards, he threw them all away and
strode off to the lift. He didn't appear in the club at all that day,
though, if he had, Mr Farthing had made up his mind to get
into conversation with him, and do a bit of spying. 'We owe it
to ourselves,' he said to himself patriotically, and he said it also
to Daphne, adding behind his hand:

'In other circumstances, I would not lower myself to speak
to a person like that. You know me.'

Daphne said she did, and laughed.

'You're only a woman,' Mr Farthing retorted. He disliked
being taken in any way but seriously. 'No wonder the country's
in the mess it is! You don't take things seriously at all!'

'I thought you said the country's mess was the fault of the
Capitalists,' she giggled and said. 'Now it's my fault!'

'I'll have a Scotch and ginger.'

'Why worry?' she said.

'I know my duty,' he said mysteriously.

'Why not join up, then?' she said, smirking.

He turned red.

'What's the good of talking to you,' he snapped, and slammed
down a florin.

He waited and watched, but Mr Bowling did not come in
at all.

Next morning, when he was opening the shop, he noticed Mr Bowling again went out and bought a lot of newspapers.

Mrs Farthing entered the shop.

Mr Farthing looked up, extremely startled.

'I thought you said you'd never set foot in this shop,' he reminded her sulkily. Then he grunted out a laugh. He'd caught her out again, she was only a woman!

She didn't mind, she was used to him.

'Dry up,' she said flatly, 'and give me a chair. I don't want to come in here, but we've got to talk.'

'Why?' he mouthed, and put a chair for her and watched her settle herself.

'The manager's just been. We can't get the rations, so we're closing the restaurant.'

He stood mouthing.

'Closing the restaurant?' He quickly feared: 'Closing this shop too? And the club?'

'Dry up, do,' she said, blowing her nose without hurry. 'I said the restaurant.' She blew her nose. 'I've decided to go down to Broadstairs with Aunt Jinnie. She wants me to help her make a go of the tea-rooms.'

They discussed it, Mr Farthing forgetting Mr Bowling temporarily. He rolled himself a fag, a habit of his, getting out fag papers, roller and tobacco, and leaning on a table, and listening to his wife.

It wasn't that Mr and Mrs Farthing disliked each other. They'd married, and things hadn't been very good financially for a long while, but they'd stuck it, running a boarding house for a bit, and then some chambers. Then his hot air got on her nerves, and things got a bit strained, but recovered somewhat when she had a baby boy, despite her crippled condition, but the boy had died, and she nearly had herself. This brought them together again, in their rough, unromantic way, her saying, Oh, dry up, to his breezy overtures about 'the old woman being a good sort, though I say it in front of her', hearty remarks like that. Then, however, on doctor's orders, she was obliged to 'refuse him the boudoir', as he called it, and he suspected the truth, which was that she was thankful for the excuse. A wall fell between them like an iron curtain, the machinery broke down and it didn't rise again. He turned against her and started having tawdry affairs with housemaids, girls in local laundries, bake houses and shops, and when his sex appeal got less and less, with prostitutes in Hyde Park and Soho. By which time, they had got the job at the Heights, and finance kept them together, on sort of semi-bitter sparring terms. Neither could now believe they had ever been anything to each other, and both were a little embarrassed at the thought of it.

They looked, as Daphne said, like a Darby and Joan gone wrong. People couldn't bear him, because of his gross ways and his great bull neck; but they liked her because of her sunny smile and the sensible way she told him to dry up.

She sat now in the shadowy shop looking rather like a queen who is graciously interviewing an old but tedious subject, who she feels she must pension off for long service. Her skirts fell round her like a crinoline, by reason of her poor, bent legs.

Mr Farthing looked not unlike a former Fascist dictator for whom the sands of time are quickly running out, and was sulky about it, but anxious to keep his end up with the Generals, for old time's sake. He might have been saying:

'Yes, it's all very well, but look what I did for Rome?'

The shop was brittle with modernness, and even the natural shadows were streaked in surrealist fashion. An arty lampshade, deeply vermilion, depicted a nude wench at the Court of King Arthur, making obeisance to the throne. King Arthur had an ultra-modern look as if he'd just had a couple at The Ivy.

A door opened into Mr Farthing's little office, and the shadow on the floor there looked as if it had been cut with a knife.

'So, that's the idea,' she said. 'So what have you got to say about that?'

His slow and sullen mind had a great deal to say, but it had been tackled too suddenly, and his thoughts had formed a bottle-neck. They bulged and strained, only little bits coming out at the moment, like, 'What's all this?' and, 'Steady on . . . what? This is all a bit . . .' and his vacant face coloured a little, telling her that he was really pleased, instinctively, at the thought of being up here on his own with Daphne, and knowing she would be making a go of the tea-rooms, where he could come flying down (God forbid) if the Heights got a bomb one night, or anything else happened. He was like a man who has been knocked very gently off his bicycle in the traffic by a Rolls Royce, knows he is not hurt, but yet wonders if he can think quickly enough so as to make a bit of money out of it, yes, look, the mudguard's a bit bent, claim a fiver for that, and, by jove, yes, look, there's a distinct bruise on my leg, small, but who's to say it might not turn into septicæmia, better put in a claim, make twenty quid out of it, *they* can afford it, Capitalists . . .

She saw all this and laughed outright.

'Dry up,' she laughed, when he said, what, clear out and leave him holding the baby? It was all very fine.

She roared with delight.

'Daph's no baby,' she cried delightedly.

He turned crimson.

'Daph? I should like to know . . . ?'

'Be your age,' she laughed at him. She blew her nose again and stopped laughing. 'Well,' she concluded pleasantly (he simply couldn't take a joke), 'so that's that.'

'Very well,' he said rather coldly. 'When are you going?'

'I'm going today. Why not? There's nothing to stop for,' she said brightly, and ignoring his act. 'I'll just put things in order, of course. And pack.'

. . . He was seeing her off in a taxi, when he saw Mr Bowling getting into a taxi too.

This depressed him very much indeed. Secretly delighted at the turn of events, he had made up his mind to concentrate very particularly on Mr Bowling, on behalf of the British Government. But when Mrs Farthing had driven cheerfully off, and had cried gaily to the driver—'Waterloo?' Mr Bowling came solemnly out of the Heights carrying a small brown suitcase, and said in that refined accent of his, 'Can you get me a taxi, porter? I want to go to Charing Cross.' There happened to be a taxi there waiting.

After some forty hours of the most acute suspense, Mr Bowling's power of endurance split in two, and with a loud and amazed laugh, to himself, he decided on his only possible course of action. He stood in his flat and exploded into a loud laugh, coming to his decision. The thing had really reached the ludicrous.

Life certainly could have the laugh of you sometimes.

The Belgian servant heard him laugh, but made no sign of any kind, and when he started to put on his hat and coat, she merely watched his lips moving, and heard him saying something or other, but her expression didn't change. She had the idea that he was leaving for good, for he went out of his way to shake hands with her, and then gave her an English five pound note. She wasn't at all sure what it was really worth, but somebody would probably tell her, and Mr Bowling saw her calmly and unemotionally take out a little purse which hung down inside her figure on a black tape, and put the note in with some others. He thought she was saving so as to start a home again after the war, when Providence permitted her to return to her native land. He smiled and said goodbye to her, nodded, picked up his suitcase and went out, thinking:

'I don't suppose she has the faintest idea what I was talking about, poor old dear, and I don't suppose she will tell the manager anything whatever—but who cares!' Outside, he saw that fellow Farthing seeing his old woman into a taxi, and watching him as usual, and he thought: 'Thank goodness I shan't have to look at that chap again, he's a positive eyesore!' The taxi-driver was bright, and he had a lot to say about the bashing the Nazis were getting in various places, and he whistled along to Charing Cross saying what he was looking forward to was when we could parachute ourselves a bit nearer Berlin itself, and knock the daylights out of the bastards.

Mr Bowling sat in the back at his ease and smiled.

Charing Cross was full of the Forces, going and coming, and he whistled his way along to the booking hall and bought a first class ticket to Knockholt.

'Single or return?' enquired the clerk.

'Single,' said Mr Bowling chirpily, good-humouredly reflecting that he would enjoy the return half on the Government.

He felt amused when he thought of the taxi-man reading his paper tonight, and when perhaps, he saw Mr Bowling's snapshot with the caption:

'Knockholt Murderer Gives Himself Up.'

The dear old chappie would push back his cap and cry:

'Blimey! Struth! . . . Jim? Fred? Come 'ere . . . look! I drove this perisher to Charin' Ruddy Cross!'

It was rather fun.

At the bookstall, Mr Bowling decided that he was tired of the newspapers, and tired of *Picture Post*, and that he would spend his time in the train in quiet contemplation. He would read a great deal of the Bible in prison, there was so much in it, the world's best seller, yet one never spared a moment to have a good go at it.

He got an empty carriage and sat in comfort, trying once again to puzzle out why on earth nothing of any kind had happened during the last forty hours. Mrs Nandle knew his address, it had been she who had written to him to ask him to come for the weekend, and although it was just possible she had completely forgotten the address, it was very unlikely. And, in any case, why had the papers not cried aloud with the Knockholt case? Granted, space was short, but there was always room for a paragraph about murder.

Finally he had come to the conclusion that she *had* lost the address, absurd though it seemed, and that she had lost his letter. 'I surely put my address on my letter?' he thought. 'I always do!' But he thought: 'Well, perhaps, for once, I didn't . . . ! But what is the matter with the police? They had only to trace my car to Godfrey Davis, who decidedly have my address and my telephone number.'

Irritated to anger, he had kicked the footstool across his sitting room, burst out laughing and exclaimed (to himself):

'B'rf! Well, my God, I'll go and bally well give myself up! Though in some ways it's a darned tame ending!'

Putting on his overcoat, he thought:

'I'll be careful about my statement, when they caution me. Counsel will insist on my pleading not guilty, and then I'll deny having given myself up at all, later. That'll pep it up a bit. Must have some fun for my money—and it'll please my public.' He was rather intrigued by the idea of having a public at last, it released a principal frustration, as he saw it. 'Composer charged with murder!' In the public eye at last—and as a composer! 'Pure vanity, of course,' he smiled to himself ruefully. 'Yet, hang it all, why on earth not, what?' He sat with his legs crossed, the crease very neatly pointed to the floor. London started to recede and blitzed buildings slipped by. The country got slowly nearer, it was a very short journey. 'These electric trains are so damn speedy,' he regretted.

The carriage door opened slowly and with difficulty, and a little girl came in from the corridor.

'Hallo,' she said coyly.

Further down the train, a working woman woke from a doze and observed that Dot was once again missing.

'That blessed, bloomin' child,' she cried, and pulled her massive body up.

She lumbered and swayed up and down the train calling:

'Doris? *Doris?*' peering in at carriages and going: 'Dot? You wait till I . . . !'

She bumped and swayed about.

Finally, she swayed into the position of being able to recount for years ahead, how Dot had the bleedin' sauce to go into a First Class carriage and sit, *if* you please, on a gen'lman's knee! There they were, like a couple of lovebirds, grinning at each other fit to kill! Oh, sir, I said, I said, sir, I do beg your pardon, I'm shaw, but that Doris'll be the death of me! And I said, fond of children, sir? . . . Sad? I never seen a man look so sad, my dear, never! None of your own, then, sir, I said, I said, well, they do have their points, but they're proper little b. . . . .s when they like, if you'll pardon my French?'

CHAPTER XV

'WHERE is the police station?' Mr Bowling enquired of a chauffeur at Knockholt.

The chauffeur told him to go straight ahead, and then to turn right, and then to turn left, and it was somewhere down there.

'Thank you,' said Mr Bowling in a subdued voice.

Something had saddened him. Perhaps it was the fact that it was such a bright day. The sky was a cold blue, and it showed up the chalk cliff there by the railway line, making you think of that sharp whiteness which summer often brought.

The fields seemed over-green and over-brown, like an excessively exaggerated painting. A horny old chap, with only one tag to his braces, was ploughing up a twisty hill.

He was enjoying this walk of his, his last in freedom for a little time, but which might seem a long time, due to impatience and inaction. It would, of course, be relieved by lively moments, and he did hope counsel for both sides would be lively and alert, and not half dead and disinterested. It would be hateful to develop into a sort of bread-and-butter case, glassy-eyed solicitors looking unimportant but pleased. Humiliating, to say the least. Rooks overhead made him think of the superstition whereby you could shout your wish to them, and they would fly off quickly and set about making it come true. Mary Webb, of course, he remembered. Then he thought of The Rookery, and wondered in which direction it lay. When he had driven down that day (how long ago? Only last Saturday?), it had been pelting with rain, and he hadn't had much idea of the outside scenery, merely shouting through the window now and again: 'I say, old boy, could you kindly tell me the way to a house called The Rookery? Mr Nandle's place?' Today the whole place seemed quite new to him, such was the frequent effect of rain. He saw the main road ahead, but had been told to turn here, and so he turned. As he walked, he said a goodbye, or an *au revoir*, for he saw life that way. 'Surely I can stick a few weeks monotony and discomfort in prison?' he argued to himself. 'And I believe gaolers, or whatever they call them, are often pretty decent fellows.' He took it easily and reached the little police station in about half an hour. He walked down a street and saw a reddish building of very unpretentious dimensions, up the road a bit, and asked a boy:

'Is that the police station, old lad?'

'Yep,' said the boy, staring with some slight interest.

'Thank you so much!'

'It's O.K.'

He felt the boy's eyes on him as he smiled and passed on with his little suitcase. He reached the police station, paused, and surveyed the entrance. 'Well,' he thought, 'goodbye to all that, it's a bit different to what I'd imagined, all this, but things usually are, and it surely isn't entirely without a spot of drama?' He said half aloud: 'I suppose one walks straight in? There's nobody about, though?' He took a bit of a deep breath, gave a last glance behind him at what the world so sadly knew as freedom, and went in.

There was nobody about.

There was a charge desk, he recognised that, because he had once taken Ivy to an Edgar Wallace play, and there had been a charge desk in that. But there had also been plenty of policemen, though one had to realise that this was the country, and not Vine Street.

As he stood there undecided, echoing footsteps were to be heard approaching, making him think of his public school, the cads were coming to rag him. It was rather funny, and his mouth went oddly dry, and he had the same tummy pain now as he had had then, when they'd trooped towards him crying:

'I know what, let's scalp that filthy cad Bowling—at him, men?' And then they would make a dive at him, and all would be arms and legs and squeals, until old Guts came in, licking his lips and saying sharply: 'At it again, Bowling? . . . Come and see me in my study in ten minutes' time? And no need to stuff your trousers—I shall examine for that!'

He felt now, when the sergeant came in with two young men in civvies, that he was going to be caned, he didn't really mind, but the sooner it was over, the better.

Then he was suddenly disconcerted to notice that the two young men were handcuffed together. One, it became clear, was a detective, and the other was a prisoner.

Mr Bowling was conscious of a slight feeling of sickness, when the sergeant turned to him and said:

'Yes? What can I do for you, sir?' in bass tones, and the two other figures in the room stood staring.

He cleared his throat. And he felt as an actor might feel, who, about to say a famous and dramatic line which, as he well knew, the audience already knew and appreciated, and wanted to hear very much indeed again, when he said in rather a quiet, dry voice:

'The name is Bowling. Bowling. I think you may be wanting to see me.'

And he managed a sad little smile. He stood waiting.

The bass voice said:

'Bowling? Oh, yes, I . . . do seem to know the name . . . !'

He looked a little embarrassed, and his eyes lit with a tiny flame of something, and he asked Mr Bowling to sit down, if he would, on the wooden bench.

Then he quickly went out of the room, calling over his shoulder: 'Take him away, Joe, and lock him up. I'll see you in a few minutes.'

The sergeant went out, Joe took the boy out and down some wooden stairs, and Mr Bowling sat sadly contemplating a faded picture of Lord Trenchard. 'I wonder,' he thought, 'will the sergeant get some commission on this?' He also thought: 'I wonder they leave me alone like this? Supposing I were to run away again?' But just then another policeman came in, said, 'good day,' in rather an embarrassed manner, gave him a long, low look and obviously pretended to be busy at the charge desk with some papers. Clearly, the sergeant had sent him in. 'Go in there, Dick, hurry,' the sergeant had probably whispered out there. 'We've got Bowling! *Bowling*, you idiot! I'll slip and fetch Chief Inspector Smith!'

But his name was Chief Inspector Thwaite.

His entrance was, to Mr Bowling, the very opposite of what he had expected. He had expected the sinister, and the bullying, and cold, calculating looks.

Chief Inspector Thwaite came very breezily in, wearing a comfortable lounge suit, shook him warmly by the hand and cried:

'Why, how nice of you to have come along, Mr Bowling—I suppose Mrs Nandle managed to get in touch with you at last, well, that's perfectly splendid . . . But what a shocking thing, poor Mr Nandle, eh—but poor Mrs Nandle too, the place being burnt to the ground like that? A terrible shock, you know,' he frowned, 'it must be, coming home from church, of all places, and finding your home, and your husband's poor body, just one mass of charred ashes? Rather makes you have a bit of a think about God?'

And he said:

'Well, let's go along to Sevenoaks and just have a chat with the two poor ladies, shall we? Routine, don't you know, and all said and done, you were the last to see the old chap alive, so far as is known?'

. . . Both Miss Souter and Mrs Nandle were exceedingly touched by the way the tragedy had upset Mr Bowling, who did not, after all, know poor Delius so well as all that. He seemed thoroughly down, and nothing that kind Inspector Thwaite could say, seemed able to make Mr Bowling see the bright side.

But people were affected differently by death, were they not? Miss Souter kept assuring Mr Bowling, as she had assured poor dear Fairy, darling Delius could not have suffered any pain. She didn't in the least believe it, and she hadn't a notion how on earth the silly man could have got himself burnt to death, when there were windows to jump out of and doors to walk through. 'Perhaps he was thinking of the blackout,' she wondered once, but it did seem that even as stupid a man as Delius must have realised that, with the house on fire, one more little light would hardly have mattered very much.

Mrs Nandle, stunned by the suddenness of the whole thing, was not in a mental condition to form any conclusion. She just knew Delius, and that the poor dear was hopeless and helpless, and she supposed he had fallen asleep and awakened to find himself surrounded by flame and smoke, perhaps half unconscious already, goodness knew the poor dear was three parts unconscious in any case.

It was a sad, affectionate little party in the hotel lounge in Sevenoaks, when Inspector Thwaite had gone. How kind he had been, and the inquest was obviously going to be a very simple and not at all an unpleasant ceremony. Both ladies wore deepest black, but Mr Bowling had evidently been too distrait to remember mourning, perhaps, and, little doubt, with the gay and sophisticated life he led in London, he didn't believe in such old-fashioned ideas. Plenty of people didn't, in fact, she had once read an article by somebody of obviously advanced and modern views, who had declared funerals should be attended in the happy atmosphere of tennis parties—'guests wearing white, and looking bright, and sucking lemonade through straws'. There was nothing white about Miss Souter and Mrs Nandle, however, except their faces, and the streaks of greyish white in their hair. They both wore black, feathery clothes, having been able to rescue a chest of clothes from the ruins, and a few items from a semi-burnt wardrobe. It was about all they did rescue, how like the blitz it was, Mrs Nandle said it reminded her of when Delius and Niggs had taken her to visit Eastcheap and Moorgate, and they had stood in the gutted ruins in the falling dusk, and felt they stood in a desolate city which God had destroyed for its sins. Poor city, it hadn't sinned, had it? And poor Delius, he hadn't sinned, not for ages—he hadn't had the chance. Or had he? The hotel lounge was dark and cosy, and the log fire there was very like the log fireplace at The Rookery. Mrs Nandle put a handkerchief to her eyes again, and peeped at the pot of beech leaves in the corner there, thinking: 'I can't bear it! To think that this must be our home now, until the insurance company pay out! I can't stand it!'

'You've still got me, dear,' Niggs patted her blackly gloved hand and said, 'You must try not to give way!' Niggs was working hard, what with trying to make Mr Bowling see the bright side, and what with trying to steer Fairy away from a further emotional breakdown (she would have it that she had not been a good wife to Delius), and what with wondering if it would look callous were she to knock back a second piece of fruit cake, it just happened to be her favourite sort. Blushing slightly, and trying to look as if she couldn't eat a thing, without it practically choking her, she snicked the coveted piece on to her plate, leaving it there for at least thirty seconds before getting down to it. 'We must *try* and see the bright side,' she told Mr Bowling in gentle tones. 'But naturally it is a dreadful shock to the three of us. And after such a jolly weekend.'

'I can't believe it,' Fairy Nandle mumured for the fortieth time. 'I just can't believe it. And when we returned home and saw the flames . . . !'

'We thought it was an enemy bomber which had been brought down, Mr Bowling. We thought it had fallen in flames in front of The Rookery. But when we got closer, it *was* The Rookery! And of course the Fire Brigade had to come such a long way.'

'They were very good,' Mrs Nandle said.

'But they could do nothing, Mr Bowling,' Niggs Souter said.

'You must come and see for yourself. Or couldn't you bear to? What do you think, Fairy, dear?'

'No! I never want to go there again! Never!'

'You must try not to give way. You still have me. Hasn't she, Mr Bowling? . . . What we cannot understand is how the fire started. Can we, dear? We think poor Delius must have fallen asleep,' she told the Coroner later in the week. She was really spokesman for Mrs Nandle, who was too overcome to be very much use in the witness box. The Coroner was such a pleasant, well-bred gentleman, they had often seen him at hunts. 'We think he must have fallen asleep,' Niggs said, 'and a spark from the fire lit the rug, the rug Mrs Nandle brought back a few years before when we all went to Egypt. The Pyramids . . .'

'Surely,' wondered the Coroner, leaning down in a kindly fashion, and ignoring the Pyramids for the time being, 'had such a thing happened, Miss Souter, one would imagine the deceased waking up almost immediately?'

'The only other theory we can think of,' Niggs thereupon said, 'was the new lamp in the scullery. It was a lamp and heater combined, and only a day or two before, Mrs Nandle had had to complain . . . had had to ask her dear husband if he would try and remember to close the front of it, it had a sliding gate.'

'Yes?'

'But we think he may have forgotten to do this, and . . .'

'Was he a forgetful man?' the Coroner rather wondered.

'I fear so,' said Miss Souter sadly and gravely. 'I don't want to say a single word against such a sweet, good . . .'

'Quite so, quite so! I appreciate that, Miss—er—Souter! But I still . . .'

'We think that something may have fallen on to this lamp, and thus the fire may have started.'

'What kind of something?'

'A dish cloth. Or . . .'

'Quite so,' frowned the Coroner, still quite puzzled, 'but surely, supposing such a thing had happened, and a fire started in the scullery, it would seem unlikely that the deceased would not be awakened? Granted that The Rookery was largely made of very old timber, it seems puzzling to me when I learn that his, er, his, er . . . that he was found on the floor of what had been the lounge, roughly at the foot of what had been the stairs?'

Miss Souter regretted that they had no other theories to offer, and she put a handkerchief to her eyes.

'Was he a man to sleep heavily, would you say?' the Coroner asked.

'Very. He would drop off on the sofa sometimes of an afternoon, and both Mrs Nandle and I would have to comp—would have to give him a jog.'

'It was difficult to rouse him?'

'Very.'

'A pity the dog was out in the kennel,' remarked the Coroner. 'Or he would have aroused him.'

'Pots would arouse anything,' Miss Souter said, adding, with slightly questionable enthusiasm, 'How thankful we are that dear *Pots* was saved, anyhow. We've got him at the hotel. They love him there.'

It seemed a rather puzzling case, but the Coroner was very used to the strange ways of men and women. He could not imagine himself snoring through a fire which had to approach from out in the scullery, and with a dog barking its head off outside in a shed; but evidently Mr Nandle had, and had become surrounded by smoke and flame, and been suffocated by fumes before he really started to get out of a sound sleep. The even odder part of it was that the evidence of the guest, Mr Bowling, who, most oddly, had been to the same public school as himself, did not clearly indicate any intentions of the deceased to have a sleep. Yes, he remembered Bowling quite well, though Bowling had been a boarder, and he had been what was disrespectfully called a Day Bug. It was quaint the way one remet people in after life. Shades of the old school, what? Mr Bowling hadn't changed at all, the same old turnip head, which he had occasionally been called, though nicknames had never stuck to him, he wasn't the popular kind. He rather liked him now, and considered him an excellent witness. Rather aloof, though, and seemingly a trifle superior, as if out of humour with life. Was he a cynic? If one remembered, he had seemed rather the idealist, as a boy? Mr Bowling's attitude rather hinted that he didn't think much of Coroners and courts. Perhaps he was just anxious to get back to town. Perhaps it was plain shyness, the ordeal of going into a witness box affected all sorts of people differently, even sophisticated people. It was often quaint.

'So then you said you would go and get the car, I suppose, Mr Bowling, and go back to town,' he suggested.

'No. I didn't say anything,' Mr Bowling said, in his cold manner.

'But the ladies went off to church. And so I suppose you indicated your intentions?'

'I certainly did that,' Mr Bowling said rather drily.

'How did he take it? What I mean is . . .'

'He took it very well.'

'What I mean to say is, was there anything in his manner to indicate that he had decided, after your departure, that he would take a nap?'

Mr Bowling pondered this.

'A nap,' he pondered.

'Yes,' the Coroner waited.

The court waited.

Mr Bowling thought, cynically: 'Well, obviously I've lost the rubber, so it doesn't matter what I say.'

So he smiled very faintly and said:

'He was lying down when I left. Like a dead'un.'

Seeing the Coroner's rather shocked expression, Mr Bowling realised that he had committed a breach of good manners.

He apologised.

'I apologise! I was not being disrespectful.'

'What you meant to say,' said the Coroner, 'was that he was actually in a recumbent position when you left him?'

'Oh, decidedly.'

'Oh, I see, well, it does seem that he was feeling tired, then, and was in fact going to have a sleep? But he didn't actually say he was going to?'

'No.'

'What did he say?'

'Say?'

'I expect he made a remark of some kind, relative to . . . ?'

'He said what about a game of draughts. I remember that.'

'*Draughts?*' said the Coroner, startled. 'Oh—so then he was *not* actually going to sleep, if . . .'

'I declined to play draughts.'

'Oh, I see! Was he on the sofa, Mr Bowling? Or . . . ?'

'When I left him he was on the floor.'

'On the *floor?*'

'Well, on the rug there.'

'But the rug was on the floor, of course . . .'

'Oh, yes! Rather!'

This was another very puzzling feature. The Coroner wondered if he ought not to recall Mrs Nandle, in order to find out if it had been the habit of the deceased to lie on the floor. But it seemed rather absurd to add to her distress by such a triviality. After all, he often lay on the floor himself, though usually he went nearer to the fire. Doubtless Mr Bowling meant he had curled up by the fire and was going to read, or something of the kind.

'He was certainly curled up, when I left him,' Mr Bowling told the court.

Back in the hotel for a final cup of tea with the two ladies, Mr Bowling seemed as dispirited as ever. But the two ladies thought him perfectly charming, he had ordered the loveliest wreath for poor Delius, and was going to stay over until tomorrow, for the funeral. The two ladies had been just a little shocked about his remark in the witness box, referring to Delius as a 'dead'un';

but, as Niggs said, he was clearly suffering from nervousness, it had been such an ordeal, and so painful for everyone. On all other occasions, Mr Bowling's manners had been flawless.

'We shall not be likely to forget you,' Niggs said to him at tea.

'No, indeed,' agreed Mrs Nandle.

'It's very charming of you to say so,' Mr Bowling said courteously. 'But I'm far from sure that I deserve it!'

'You do deserve it,' Niggs said. 'And we do so hope you won't let it get you down. We have all got to go some day, I don't expect you have ever looked at it that way,' she smiled sadly. 'But you *must* try and see the bright side!'

CHAPTER XVI

THE two ladies talked for a little, in droning voices, rather like two bees who were quite unable to leave the vicinity of, say, a marrow bed; it was beginning to smell a bit, but there was still an unusual sweetness which lingered; the item of poor Delius being so utterly charred, unrecognisable except for his wrist-watch, which had had a steel clasp, Fairy had given it to him for his recent birthday; and the item of not being able to find Mr Bowling, 'so stupid of us, but your letter got burnt,' Mrs Nandle explained, 'and Niggs quite thought the flats were called Madison Flights, or Madison Flats, and she said it was in W6. That was why you didn't get the letter.' Then Mrs Nandle suddenly stopped and stared. Mr Bowling had said he had not had the letter, how, then, had Mr Thwaite found him? Truly the police were wonderful. Perhaps the wireless had sent out a police message. Well, it was all over now. Except for the funeral.

'We shall see you at the funeral,' Mrs Nandle shook hands with Mr Bowling. She gave a sad little smile.

'Yes,' he bowed.

'Cheerio,' said Miss Souter, in the modern manner she adopted at times. 'We shall see you?'

He bowed and smiled sadly.

'Yes.'

But he didn't see them again.

He went upstairs.

Going to his room, he felt a sense of despondency and gloom, and although he recognised his moods, now, he thought the present one was at any rate in part caused by the darkness of the hotel. It was low-ceilinged, and the rooms and passages were black-beamed and narrow, there wasn't nearly enough light. He suddenly decided that he could not stick it any longer, and that he was very much afraid he would not wait for the funeral after all. 'I'll write a polite note to the poor old dears,' he decided, 'and say I'll not be able to stay after all, I have to get back to jolly old London.' He stood in his dark bedroom, evening shadows starting to fall. The door he had left open was creaking a little as it rode to and fro, in a strong draught. Somebody was moving about in the room bang opposite, and a girl's voice was humming briskly an old song something about 'Hot Sock Roleson, On the river bank, and a bowl of steaming suet', and he wished she'd get the words right, he was quite sure they weren't that. He sat at a writing table, staring at paper and pens, aware that it was almost too much effort to pick up a pen and put:

'My dear Mrs Nandle,
    I find that it is necessary for me to get back to London at once, and I do hope you won't think it unkind of me not to attend the funeral tomorrow. My thoughts will be with you both the whole of the day. This is a very sad world, and it never seems to work out according to plan, now it is full of deepest sorrow, now it is quite ludicrously gay. I can only hope your sorrow will grow into a happy memory, and will become fragrant as rosemary on a summer evening. Love is the great thing, is it not, and you are a thousand times blessed to have experienced it at all. I know Delius would share these thoughts with me. My kindest thoughts to Miss Souter. I am more than happy to think you can never be alone while she is with us— which I pray will be for many a long day yet.'

His thoughts broke for a bit, on account of the rather sacrilegious thought that Delius had been such a complete twerp, and on account of the thought that dear Niggs couldn't possibly live much longer, she must surely be deep in her sixties. So he finished abruptly: 'With kindest regards, Yours sincerely, W. Bowling.' The sound of *Hot Sock Roleson* grew a little nearer, and stopped just over his shoulder. He started and looked round.

She was the slimmest and loveliest woman he had ever set eyes on, and when he looked into her eyes he thought of milk. She wasn't an adolescent, but he thought of adolescence, and couldn't take his eyes off her. Her hair hung down in a flat, sophisticated, netted fashion, and she had green ear-rings. The only other thing he noticed about her was the smell of her. He had had the same feminine sensation in his nostrils during the blitz, when a bomb blew up a scented soap factory. Standing in the dark there, and getting the scent of it, it lingered. She wanted something or other, he didn't even hear what it was. She was polite but perky and she knew all about her beauty and what her eyes did to men in buses and undergrounds and cafés and dance halls and ballrooms and stately homes of England. He became aware that he was trying to delude himself that it had happened at last, and already his lips framed the word: 'Angel?' He prayed passionately: 'If only she refuses me—then it's Angel,' even though he knew that she had touched his life too late; he was not merely a wash-out now: everyone must consider him evil, even if he didn't consider it himself?

But even as the seconds ticked over, and now he wanted it to be Angel, and now he didn't, and even as they stood there in the tumbling shadows, he knew she was just another woman, with just another story, which worried her secretly. Illusion fell away, like fantasy which has been ruined by somebody chucking a brick into the window of a pantomime and letting forth cockney oaths at the princess in her golden coach.

He went for her, because he wanted her, and because he thought there was a chance she might raise a shindy about it.

But she didn't.

Neither of them even thought of shutting the door, until after.

*

He shut it and went back and lay on the bed beside her. Her hair had got loose, it was white as silk, like a faded buttercup. She was rather like a buttercup herself.

She had a matter-of-fact voice.

'I'm sorry about it,' she said, meaning something private concerning them.

'It's all right, my dear,' he told her pleasantly.

'You are a nuisance!'

'The sensation's mutual!' He gave a little laugh.

She lay flat and said:

'I've lied to you. I said I wasn't married. I am.'

He didn't say anything for a moment. Then he said:

'I'm sorry to hear that. I would not have . . .'

'Men always pretend that,' she interrupted sharply.

'I think I mean it. I'm dead against adultery. Honestly. I don't say I've never committed adultery, I have. But I was young and I was learning.'

'Did it need many lessons?' she asked.

'No,' he said seriously.

She said:

'My husband and I love each other. I know that. But we don't get on. I can't tell you why, it's too intimate. I was very young indeed when we married, I was at school . . . He's gone back East, and it's best for him, he gets what he wants out there, and needn't bother me. I'm in the Hell of a mess,' she said.

'Yes, you are. What's your name?'

'My christian name is Heather. It doesn't matter about the rest.'

'We shan't meet again, anyway. Except by a fluke.'

'No, I know.'

'What are you doing here, Heather?'

'I wish I knew. He went yesterday, and I had a nausea against London, got out the car and hared down here. I've no plans whatever.'

'You'd better make some.'

'Oh, I will! I'm having a think. I'm thinking of divorce, all sorts of things. I can go home, I suppose. What are your plans?'

He thought and then said slowly:

'I think I'm going to have just one more shot at achieving a certain something I've been trying bally hard to achieve for some little time.'

'What's that?'

'It's too intimate to tell you. Or, rather, you'd never believe me if I did tell you.'

'I would . . .'

'No! You wouldn't! There's only one person in the world who would understand.'

'Who?' she turned on her side and said. She was interested in him.

'I call her Angel,' he said shyly.

'That's nice,' she said. 'Where does she hang out?'

He turned to her and smiled sorrowfully.

'I'm blessed if I know,' he sighed. He laughed again. 'I haven't met her yet.'

She turned over on her back again.

'You're kidding,' she said, disappointed. 'I thought you were serious.'

Yet, goodness knew, he looked serious enough.

Presently, she lay looking up at him. His eyes were steel grey, and extremely strong. They shone strength. Humour tinged the creases round his eyes and mouth. His mouth wasn't strong, but it was very fine and she liked it. As in all the men she saw, one side of his face expressed hidden good, and the other side hidden evil. If a human being was a silent battle between the two, she would have judged that the good side was leading by inches. When he loved her, he seemed to be pleading, as well as fighting, and he seemed to want to draw out of her a spiritual something which she was fully aware was not in her power to give, it was comprised of heart and brain and soul, whereas she knew only too well that she was principally body. Well, at any rate she could give him that—which she did, until she cried.

He was panting.

'Don't cry, for God's sake,' he pleaded.

But she cried.

'I'm sorry!'

'Tears,' he said, obscurely. 'Heck, I'm going to dress!'

She lay in disarray and blew her nose. The draught from the window touched her skin at many points, and downstairs the gong started up for dinner.

'What an old-fashioned sound,' she said.

. . . It had cleared his brain; and although he didn't regard it as love, he recognised its physical value: the scales had slipped from the backs of his eyes once again, and for a very little time indeed would remain slipped away.

Then the little black velvet curtain would steal quietly down again.

He hired a chauffeur to take him back to town, and he sat in the back thinking about her. In an hour or two he would never think of her again; and quite likely she would never think of him. She said she'd done it before, now and then, how could she help it, with eyes like that? On his knee was a copy of the *Kent and Sussex Courier*. It was too dark to read now, but he had already glanced through the paragraph which said a verdict of accidental death had been returned at the inquest this afternoon on Delius Nandle, late of The Rookery, Knockholt, which had been burnt to the ground on Sunday night. And it said that Delius Nandle would be heartily missed by his many friends, and most particularly would they miss him at The Drill Hall on Wednesday nights, where he had taken the keenest interest in the whist drives. It said that Knockholt extended the greatest sympathy to the widow, 'and to Miss Souter whose relations are so well known in connection with the relief of Ladysmith.' On the advertisement page it said that there were ferrets for sale at Cumber Cottage, apply Mr Dridges personally between two and four any afternoon. It was nice.

Mr Bowling sat thinking about the immediate future. There was that in his face which was intensely resolute, and that in it which was good-humoured—rather as a man might look who was thinking: 'You'd still try and fool me, would you?' and looking knowing about it. 'We shall now bally well see,' his genial but determined look said. It was really past being laughable.

'I'm getting a bit browned off,' he thought once, and lit a cigar.

The swiftly changing thoughts in his mind all of a sudden pounced on a queer little item.

'By *jove*!' he exclaimed, almost aloud. 'I clean forgot it! And so did she!'

He had thought of the little parcel marked 'fragile' which he had promised to deliver for Mrs Nandle to a friend of hers in Brook Green. He had shoved it down somewhere in the flat and clean forgotten all about it.

When he came to considering the importance of that little matter, (which he was going to come to very soon indeed), he found it absorbing, being ever of the turn of mind which says, there, if I hadn't gone to see the So-and-So's, I'd never have met So-and-So; but for the moment he merely thought: 'How very remiss of me! I must get on a bus this evening and tootle along with it!'

In the same way, he was very soon indeed to come to considering the matter of Mr Farthing.

For the present, had anyone said, Oh, you remember old Farthing, who runs that shop affair at the Heights?—he would not have had the remotest idea who they were talking about.

And even when the car drew up once again at the Heights, and he saw Mr Farthing interestedly watching him, he could honestly declare: 'My dear chap, at that moment I never had the slightest idea that he was to be my next victim, I never gave him the slightest thought!'

And yet, how obvious, it later seemed, that he should murder Mr Farthing.

The fellow was *made* for murder.

'By jove, yes,' he thought then. 'What an ass I've been! I ought to have bumped him off weeks ago . . . ! And in the matter of getting caught there, I could hardly make an error this time! The fellow weighs fifteen stone, and would most certainly quickly be missed?'

He also thought:

'Another thing: a chap like that would be sure to put up a pretty good struggle. He's no doubt got lungs like an elephant. It ought to add a bit of sportsmanship and spice. I shouldn't really care to be accused of not playing cricket!'

When he entered the flats, a porter dashed up to take his suit-case—it was all so pleasant. He had that homing feeling, liking the action, the colour and the lights; and the sensation only dimmed very slightly when he went into his flat and switched on the lights. He quickly had to switch them off again, for the blackout had to be done. The porter helped him and remarked:

'Mr Clark thought you weren't coming back, sir. I think he's letting the flat.'

He remembered that he had tried to tell the Belgian he was not coming back, and evidently she had tumbled to it.

'Well,' he said, 'I shall be here for a day or two. So will you tell Mr Clark?'

Mr Clark was the manager. The porter went and told Mr Clark, returning with the message that Mr Clark would be pleased to get the matter quite clear.

'Quite clear,' pondered Mr Bowling aimiably. He mixed a whisky and soda and sat down with it.

The porter was a young chap and looked like a friendly bulldog.

'Yes, sir, Mr Clark couldn't make out why you left your things, sir, I think that was it. Rent was paid up ahead too, sir. That's a very unusual thing here. I don't think Mr Clark quite understood, sir.'

'I see,' said Mr Bowling chirpily.

The porter said:

'He said he'd take the liberty of calling on you during the late evening, sir, if that would be convenient?'

'It would be quite convenient, old chap. Tell him to pop in any old time. If I'm out, I shan't be many minutes, just going to pop along to Brook Green. By the way, how do I get there?'

The porter had long arms which hung down. He said if it was him, he'd walk to Brook Green.

Then he volunteered the news that he'd had his call up papers, and was going into the Navy.

'Splendid,' said Mr Bowling.

'Signallers.'

'Excellent! I congratulate you!'

'I passed my medical. They didn't half mess me about.'

'They messed me about, too!'

'There was nothing they didn't think of. But you get used to it, don't you, sir? We were all in the same boat. But I don't think I should care to be them doctors, would you? Staring all day at that sort of thing?'

Mr Bowling said it would not appeal to him at all.

'No, sir.'

'You must have a drink before you go, we must drink to your success in the Navy!'

The boy shook his head.

'Thanks all the same, sir. I promised mum I'd never touch it, and I'm never going to!'

'Well, you know best. I wish you all the luck in the world.'

'Thank you, sir. Well, I'll tell Mr Clark he can come up.'

'Do.'

He tipped the boy and he went out looking very pleased. Mr Bowling felt in genial, if slightly lonely, mood, and wandered about trying to find the little parcel which Mrs Nandle had entrusted him with. He found it in his bedroom on the dressing table, just as he had left it. Mrs Nandle's large handwriting said: 'Miss Mason, 66 Brook Green, London, W6.' Brook Green he knew as the rectangular piece of grass and hard tennis courts which lay between Hammersmith and Shepherds Bush, and was hardly ten minutes' walk from the Heights, if you knew that part of London. He would go along there presently, after he had had something to eat somewhere. There was a French restaurant in Notting Hill Gate, and he thought he would eat there. But it was a little late, in these war days, and the place might be shut. It was half-past eight. He sat down at the piano and played some Chopin for a little while, and was just thinking of knocking off when the door bell rang. He wandered whistling to the door and was not a little surprised to find Mr Farthing standing there.

He stopped whistling. What on earth did this fellow want?

'Good evening?' he said civilly.

CHAPTER XVII

MR FARTHING thought it a bright idea of his, to start the Paper Salvage campaign. He tackled anybody who was in on Mr Bowling's floor, succeeding in getting promises from old Cooker, retired Indian civil servant, who had a one-room flat next to Bowling, and from the Misses Phelps, two sisters who were opposite. He made every effort to be charming, an effort which did not change his appearance particularly, but which slightly removed some of his permanent scowl.

'Thank you very much,' he told the Phelps, peering in at their flat to see if there was anything of interest. He often wondered whether the Misses Phelps went in for slap and tickle, they weren't old, and the airs they gave themselves might easily have been camouflage. Mr Farthing had never forgotten the time he had undertaken to mend a window catch for a lady who, as he put it, was *actually titled*, though she went about incognito, and who had had a very tasty flat on the top floor. He went in to mend this window catch, and had had a very nice chat with madam, and then turned round suddenly to find she was on the sofa, 'stark naked, it's as true as I'm standing here,' he told many a man in the club. 'I leave the rest to you!' He had felt very proud. Since then, he always rang flat bells with a certain sense of anticipation. The Misses Phelps, however, had no time for him whatever, though they were glad to agree to put out any spare paper in a separate heap in the passage every morning. 'Thank you very much,' Mr Farthing said, and the door shut rather firmly in his face. 'Bleeding Capitalists,' he decided, and went along to old Cooker's door and pressed the buzzer.

Old Cooker came to the door. He was delighted to see anyone, even Farthing, for he was one of the loneliest men in London. London was so unfriendly. He had called on his new neighbour a number of times, a Mr Bowling he gathered from the porter, but either he was always out, or he didn't bother to answer the bell, which was what so many people did. It was a pity, because he could hear him playing the piano, and Mr Cooker was known in Punjhab as being 'musical. His aunt once met Dame Melba, you know.'

Mr Cooker's one-room flat was in an unholy mess, Mr Farthing staring disgustedly at saucepans and plates and cups, unwashed, on ends of chairs, and on bookcases, and on Cooker's photograph album. Cooker's photograph album was one of the most frightening things in the Heights. He at one time used to bring it down to the club, and it was the direct cause of him being the only Life Member to be expelled (under Rule 62b, see Club Rules) which clearly and painfully indicated that, 'Whereas, and as whereunder, the member aforementioned, having been proved to the satisfaction of the Committee, *and at least three independent witnesses*, to have been a nuisance to other members *on more than two occasions*, could be peremptorily expelled from the aforementioned club, by letter.' There had been an endless stream of eager witnesses, who had spent days ringing up the Secretary and enquiring brutally, 'Look here, what are we going to do about Cooker, he's pestering people with that bloody album again?' And whereas the offence had been committed on positive divers occasions, let alone two or three, a very sharp letter was written, and taken out, and publicly posted in the letter box outside, just in case delivery by hand made for an infringement of the law, and gave the old boy a loophole, which he certainly searched for with all speed and avidity. Failing to find one, however, Mr Cooker told the Secretary, 'straight from the shoulder,' that the country was going to the dogs, and small wonder, with the types that got about nowadays! He took his album upstairs to his flat and vowed never to join a club again. Seeing the album Mr Farthing thought he had made a marvellous coup for his Salvage Campaign, but didn't mention it, in case Cooker lured him in and started going: 'Yes, I knew you'd be interested in that—and this is a tiger I

bagged in '05, see that tree? Well, a little to the right of it is me!'
And: 'Now, this was taken by my dear wife, it's on the Governor
General's estate! Stop me if I've told you this before, I don't think
I have, but they say I repeat myself? Well, this particular bag . . .'
As it was, Mr Cooker was standing holding a frying pan, and
wearing a little red cap with a tassel. He asked Mr Farthing in,
notwithstanding his connections with the club, for the quarrel
had been just before Mr Farthing had taken over the job. Firmly
refusing, Mr Farthing said, no, no thank you, he didn't intend to
interrupt Mr Cooker's meal—it seemed difficult to call it 'dinner,'
seeing that it was so spread out, in Eastern fashion, as it were,
Sultan Cooker, preparing to squat on the floor and eat from there,
there was a pie on the tuffet, and some brown bread and butter
on the floor itself, near the radiator. 'I'm dining alone,' said Mr
Cooker, 'and you are most welcome to share my humble repast?
I have dined with kings and commoners, but I am never so happy
as when entertaining in my own home.'

'Capitalists?' queried Mr Farthing, not quite catching the word
commoner, and wondering what Mr Cooker meant by kings and
Capitalists, which were so deplorably one and the same thing.
'Don't talk to me about Capitalists! No, sir! No, what I've just
popped in about, is not to interrupt your, er . . . food. It's just
about waste paper, Mr Cooker. I shall be very glad to collect any
you put out each day. It's for the war effort, you know.'

'I shall be delighted,' said Mr Cooker, and at once put down
his frying pan and started collecting newspapers.

'I didn't mean now,' Mr Farthing said, backing away carefully.
'I just thought I'd start asking folks.'

'My dear sir, it's a perfectly splendid and most patriotic idea
and . . .'

'It's not that I'm helping win the war for Capitalism, please
don't think that? I just don't like the idea of being in chains.'

'Chains?'

'The only mercy likely to be shown if the hordes get here,
will be mercy to fair headed Scotsmen. Well, *I* don't happen

to be a Scot!' Mr Farthing had got it all worked out. 'I shall jump off the building, I think. Might just as well.'

Mr Cooker expressed astonishment at his attitude, and grew rather fiery, going, 'But, my dear sir,' in scandalised tones, his tassel bobbing about over his scarlet forehead.

'Well,' explained Mr Farthing, tapping his sloping forehead, 'you want it up here, don't you? That's where you want it, Mr Cooker!'

'Up there?' stared the other's piggy eyes. 'But, my dear sir . . . !'

'Oh, I know what they all say here about me,' Mr Farthing said darkly. 'Why aren't I in the Army? Or the Air Force! Or the Navy! Or the Civil Defence! And why aren't I a conchie?' He sucked his teeth. 'They'd like to know how I got reserved, I daresay! Yes, I daresay they would!'

Mr Cooker's mind chased after him. He was not very quick, and Mr Farthing kept dodging from one thing to the next, it was impossible to keep pace. Now he was talking about Mr Bowling.

Or was he talking about Capitalism again?

'I'm going to see him now,' Mr Farthing was now saying.

'Who?' mouthed Mr Cooker, like an old dog catching up with the scent. 'Oh you mean my neighbour, Mr . . .'

'There's quite a lot of people in civvies in this country! Quite a lot! And I daresay some of them would not bear too close an enquiry, if one faced up to it, what-say?'

'What-say,' repeated Mr Cooker, groping. 'What . . . ?'

'So I'll be getting along, Mr Cooker. Sorry to have troubled you?'

'What? Trouble? Not at all, won't . . . ?'

'Another time, thank you very much, I've had my dinner, in any case. Goodnight, sir!'

Mr Farthing walked firmly away.

Mr Cooker stared after him, returned muttering and closed his door.

Mr Farthing walked quietly along the blue matted carpet and

stopped in front of Mr Bowling's door. He listened for a moment. Mr Bowling was playing the piano.

He put a square thumb on the buzzer and pressed. It went: *Bzzzzzzzz*.

The music stopped and an inner door opened. The sound of Mr Bowling whistling *Hot Sock Roleson* grew nearer and nearer.

The door opened.

. . . The relative, and relevant, verbal and factual details, immediately leading to the moment when, with back bent like a broad and tightly padded arc of steel, Mr Bowling judged it time to place a huge and iron hand hard down on the back of Mr Farthing's neck, thereby inducing in him, perhaps for the first time in his life, an attitude of prayer, are not of vital interest, unless of time-passing, purely: for it might be said of another—well, it doesn't matter what he *said*, the point is he found himself on the live rail, and the sparks started to fly. For Mr Bowling knew, by then—and, indeed, he knew it when Mr Farthing stood there in the doorway—that for Mr Farthing the plum was ready to drop. He smacked his hand down hard, shoving that immense head well down between the knees, then quickly inserting the other hand in the hollow made, and warmly covering Mr Farthing's nose and mouth. Mr Farthing let out a nasal squeal which was stillborn, and gave an astonished plunge forward, his arms like buttresses. Amused, and reddening under the strain, Mr Bowling exerted his strength, tightly gripping the mouth and nose still, and keeping the head well down, and he allowed play and backed under pressure to the brown curtains. He puffed good-naturedly and thought: 'Now, this is not because you told me the name of a woman here you'd had relations with, and it is not because I think that sort of thing particularly caddish.

'And nor is it because I happen to want an excuse to kill someone. It's—well, just because you came here, and Destiny brought you saying: Your Time is Now and There—go in!'

Mr Farthing on the other hand, was thinking along a totally different plane: it was not that he wanted to come in and talk to this fellow Bowling, whom he despised utterly for what he appeared to be, and doubtless was, to wit, a snob, and a filthy Capitalist, and quite probably a Fifth Columnist, and above all a person contemptuous of persons like himself. True, it was not considered very nice to say you had raped a woman, if you were also going to say that woman's name. Admitted, that was a slip, but Mr Bowling had put on such superior airs, that bloody accent of his, and his nonchalant and contemptuous manner, and had had the unmerited cheek to say he, Farthing, was a Capitalist. What had led up to that? Why, seeing the airs Bowling was giving himself, he'd mentioned a bank account, not to be out-done, and Bowling had sneered: 'Ha—bally Capitalist, what? Eh, Farthing?' It had been a shock. *Me* a Capitalist! Gracious! And what had led up to that? Why, chatter about people. He'd tried to be genial to Bowling, had managed to gain entry, reluctant though the invitation sounded, had accepted a drop of gin, had finished with paper salvage, and had started on 'people'. Mr Farthing had said he didn't think Mr Bowling was a very sociable kind. 'Perhaps you don't like people,' he commented, trying to be nice-sounding, but eyes all the time working on behalf of the British Government. The man seemed to have plenty of money, he'd got comforts of every kind, even a bottle of Bols. There were no photographs, which was interesting, and rather curious, surely, was he married or engaged or anything? Did he keep a woman? Or what did he do in that line? The conversation became, at Mr Farthing's instigation, though he had not intended it, the kind of interview in which the visitor says one thing, and the host goes one better; and then the visitor senses a hostility and goes one better still. At last, frozen smiles fade altogether, and remarks become more open, rather hackneyed, because the one is thinking: 'What shall I ask Mr Bowling next, shall I ask him point blank what he's doing here at the Heights?' and the other is thinking: 'This fellow is getting very inquisitive? Why exactly has he come here? It was surely a little rash of him?' When Mr Bowling got up and said: 'I don't think that's any of your affair, Farthing,' not even saying 'Mr' Farthing now, to a perfectly careful question about where he had lived before he came to the Heights, Mr Farthing's aggressive chin threw out a distinct challenge. But he wasn't quite ready for open warfare for a minute or two, and he sideskirted on to the ever-ready topic of woman, and found himself in startlingly deep water. He had once insulted his mother, as a youth, and he had done it thoughtlessly, and the same atmospherical sense of pending calamity was felt then, as now; he too had sown the wind, and had reaped the whirlwind: mother had crowned him with an iron stewpot and knocked him senseless for several minutes.

As now, although not senseless, a similar and very great amazement happened, directly after Mr Bowling remarked so very calmly:

'I don't think we need all this light,' and a hand had gone to a switch.

Very large hands they were, noticed Mr Farthing, who was sitting in a forward position in the armchair, facing the velvet curtains.

He suddenly received an unbelievably astonishing, and smarting, smack on the back of the neck.

An enormous weight pressed his head right down into his crutch, and another rude hand inserted its suffocating self over his mouth and nose.

For an eternity of time, which was not really so long as a second, Mr Farthing told himself and his outraged body, that this truly astounding indignity was not and could not be real, he was imagining it.

But he also knew that it was real. It was very real indeed.

'This man,' he thought, 'must be a maniac?'

He exerted all his considerable strength and shoved. He also put out two blind arms and got a good if strained grip on Mr

Bowling's calves. But he could not hold him there, the man was like a snake and had slipped still further behind him.

Mr Bowling was what he called piggy-back, sprawled across Mr Farthing's huge shoulders, one hand still tightly about his mouth and nostrils, and the other, now, under his chin. He pulled steadily back, using his left knee as leverage.

Mr Farthing let out another nasal squeal, but was forced back, back, back.

He twisted, however, and gave a violent wrench; there was a loud noise of smashing glass and crockery.

Next door, Mr Cooker started.

Whenever Mr Cooker heard anything, he always thought it was guns. And he always liked to hurry to his door and go out into the passage. There might be somebody there to whom he could say:

'Have the sirens gone? I thought I heard guns?'

He would then make a tremendous business of getting out a pink mattress and blankets, in preparation for sleeping in the passage all night. He was not nervous, but there were people to talk to, he adored the blitz.

He opened his door sharply and stood peering up and down. There was nobody about, but he heard another thump, either of guns, or of something falling over with a crash in Mr Bowling's flat.

He went along and peered through Mr Bowling's letter-box.

He saw a very dim light, as if only the fire was on, it was shining through the glazed inner door. He listened, thinking he heard the sound of heavy breathing.

Finally, however, he decided he was quite mistaken. It must have been guns.

He went all the way down to the lounge to ask.

No, it was not guns. But still, it had passed ten minutes.

He could go to bed reasonably soon.

He went back.

No sooner had he got back, but he thought he heard another sound of breaking glass, a window or something. He sat irritatedly chewing his nails. Life was very sickening. So many things went on, and you never knew what it was. He might be missing a murder! He gave a deep sigh and sat on the bed.

Mr Bowling gave a deep sigh and sat on the floor. He tried to get a better purchase, to rest his aching arms. Presently he managed to slide himself and Farthing nearer to the wall, where he got a good grip with his feet on the sofa-back. The sofa slid a little way and then very conveniently stopped. Farthing was like an old Spanish bull. He just wouldn't die. Mr Bowling had two hands clasped about his ugly mouth, and he had his head bent well backwards so that, in an upside down manner, he could stare into the hatred and terror which those inverted eyes threw up at him. Mr Farthing's hard work with his own two hands was beginning to die down a bit. There was a strong smell of sweat, and there was a filthy mess of blood. Mr Bowling had tumbled a nasty one against the corner of the table, and had cut the left temple open. Blood was everywhere. Mr Farthing's legs writhed and twisted in agony. The pink colour of his mind had started to turn black. Very suddenly indeed, without having really enjoyed any consecutive or constructive thought at all, something in his pained vision threw a piece of black cloth; and his heavy body relaxed, limp.

After a little time, Mr Bowling got up and tottered into the bathroom.

CHAPTER XVIII

HE took off his jacket and turned on the cold tap. There was the cool sound of it trickling into the basin, and he bathed his cut head and thought: 'Phew, I'm bally hot, what? If I have to do any more of these murders—which God forbid—I think I shall just wear a singlet and flannels. Shorts would really be best,' he thought, soaping his immense biceps. He dried his face, but the cut was still bleeding, and was the swollen colour of a new bruise. He got a bit of cotton wool out of the little cupboard, and shoved it on, he was clumsy at such things. Then he found a bit of plaster. He had just washed and dried his hands again, and was doing up the cuff links which Queenie had given him—they were a ball and bat, very natty, done in flattened gold—when he heard a distinct sound in the passage behind him. He swung round. Like a half dead rat with only the petrified instinct to make a dash for it, broken limbs and all, Mr Farthing had come round again and was plunging silently to the door. He had reached the door by the exact time the old dog's nose again sniffed him, and he let out that nasal squeal of his and started lashing out with both fists like a man in a nightmare. His baboon-like face was contorted with prayerful terror, mouth open like a haunted child, huge back thumping the door as he hit out. Mr Bowling felt extremely irritated. He had received two upper cuts, and a sock in the guts, so off his guard had he been—when before had the dead presumed to come to life? But he was an intelligent man, and always used his brain before he used anything else, and his mind slipped back to the old school quad, where the Sergeant Major had put him through his paces after O.T.C. 'Keep out the left, my lad—and let 'im 'ave it with yer right . . . so!' So—had always meant a sharp smack in the teeth for Mr Bowling, he now remembered, and he now remembered all sorts of little tips concerning the great art of boxing. It was, indeed, shadow boxing, for it was nearly dark in the hall, and he could only hit at the darkest parts, which were probably Mr Farthing. He hit hard and often, sometimes taking a sharp one back, nearly always below the belt.

Mr Farthing was breathing, squealing and whimpering, and there was that fusion of, and outward manifestation of, breathless speech, which now and then sounded like . . . *police? help? . . . murder?* Mr Farthing's one idea was to keep the man at a distance, he dreaded beyond all things the grip of those suffocating hands. He started to squeal again, but suddenly got a nasty one on the tip of the jaw, it sounded like—*clak.* It knocked the daylights out of him. Mr Bowling noticed the shadow which was Mr Farthing heel over somewhere, and he heard him fall. He had observed the sound *clak* too, with a certain amount of pride, and yet with the sensation that it was not the collision of his fist on the other's jaw. It was another kind of *clak*, like something pretty tough snapping in two. He groped about and bent over Mr Farthing, who was huddled in the doorway to the bedroom. As he did so, somebody opened the letter-box, a blurred face peered through and a petulant voice said:

'Who's there? . . . Is anybody in there?'

Mr Cooker peered into the semi-darkness. There was this time a light in Mr Bowling's bathroom, and although the bathroom door was half shut, a glimmer came through into the little hall. He was perfectly sure there was a burglar messing about in Bowling's flat. All that thumping, and other peculiar sounds, and then sounds like somebody crying, or whatever it was.

Mr Cooker stood holding a blunderbuss which his father had used in the Crimea. It had two huge hammers, and they were at the ready. In a stern if quavery voice, he called through the letter-box:

'Come along, the game's up?' forgetting that the door was firmly locked between him and his enemy. 'Who is there, come along, now?' he trembled. His little tassle shook over his forehead, and he looked like a peevish frog.

There was dead silence in Mr Bowling's flat.

Mr Cooker decided to say through the letter-box:

'I shall wait here until you give yourself up,' but in reality to tiptoe downstairs to the manager.

This he did, taking his blunderbuss with him. He knew the manager didn't like him, but burglars were burglars, and were tenants entitled to their protection, or were they not?

He went downstairs. The manager, however, was not to be found. He was doing the round of some of the flats. The porters all laughed at Mr Cooker, and looked slightly embarrassed, refusing firmly to be dragged upstairs.

'You imagine things, sir,' they sniggered, staring at his blunderbuss.

One of them told him that the manager was calling on Mr Bowling presently, in any case. 'He's doing the rounds now,' he said.

Mr Cooker mouthed.

'Lot of ignoramuses,' he snapped.

'Burglars can't get in the flats, Mr Cooker,' the head porter said comfortably. 'Especially on the upstairs floors, where there's a sheer drop on to the concrete! And the only person to use a pass key to the flats is the manager—Mr Clark!'

They all yawned at Mr Cooker, and sniggered when he stamped off upstairs again.

'Poor old beggar,' they sniggered.

Mr Bowling stepped over Mr Farthing—or, rather, the late Mr Farthing—whenever he went from his bedroom to the bathroom and back. He regretted to observe that Mr Farthing had died from a broken neck. Well, it made a change, but there was nothing to be depressed about, it was still murder, wasn't it?

He had put on all the lights.

The sitting room was in an unholy mess, the table on its side, a tray of decanters and glasses in ruins on the floor, the standard lamp on its side and smashed, and a glass panel knocked out of the sitting room door.

He had suddenly remembered that Mr Clark, the manager, was calling on him this evening. It wouldn't do to have the place so untidy. However, he did feel he must have some air, and he had still had nothing to eat. He really must tootle out and have a spot up at the Coach and Horses, a plate of beef, perhaps. He also really ought to pull himself together and take the little parcel to the address in Brook Green, it would soon be getting rather late.

He put on his overcoat and brown felt hat and turned out the lights. He stepped over the late Mr Farthing and went out, slamming the door. He then became aware that his neighbour was standing there, what was his name, holding a bally blunderbuss. He then realised who it must have been peering so inquisitively through the letter-box.

'Excuse me, sir,' exclaimed Mr Cooker, looking his astonishment. 'Have you been in long?' He stared at the plaster on Mr Bowling's left temple.

'In?' queried Mr Bowling politely. 'In where, old man?'

'In your flat, sir . . . ?'

'Yes, rather!'

'Well, sir, you must forgive my seeming inquisitiveness, but the fact is I thought I heard noises, and . . . !'

Mr Bowling interrupted. He was rather charming.

He touched Mr Cooker's shoulder and laughed ruefully.

'I thought I heard noises myself, sir! And when I was having a look round, I fell and banged my jolly old head on the corner of the table!'

He walked away, his laugh trailing away with him to the lifts. Mr Cooker called:

'But, dear me, sir, we should continue searching, this burglar may be on your balcony, or . . . ? I shall speak to Mr Clark, sir,' he promised.

'Don't bother,' called Mr Bowling. 'I'll speak to him myself when I get back. I shan't be long.' He went down in one of the lifts and thought: 'I think a rather interesting little plan might be to pick up Mr Clark when I get back, and we could enter the flat together. What would a jury think of that? It would make the trial interesting, what? And with my blood on both our suits, and this cut on the head—I should hardly be likely to get away with it?' He stood in the lift, going down, down, his left hand on the little parcel in his pocket for Miss Mason. He went along to Notting Hill Gate to eat, had some draught beer and walked down the hill again to Brook Green. He found Number Sixty-six as a London clock was distantly chiming ten.

He stood in the darkness and put on a Gold Flake. The night was excitingly cold, it was as if a man had stepped out of a cold bath into the moonlight. There was a brand new moon, and it was like the light from a blowlamp, so vivid was it, you needed an eye shield.

Number Sixty-six looked like some kind of house turned hostelry for girls. The front door had a brass plate which was in the shadows and impossible to read. The front door was wide upon. There was a night light back in the hall, on a table which held flowers of some kind, it was too dark to see. When he reviewed this moment later, Mr Bowling told himself that he did have an intuition concerning the greatness of this moment; but then, one often did that—afterwards?

He found an old fashioned bell-pull and gave it a tug.

It came away in his hand.

He tossed away his cigarette and laughed lightly. 'Struth, what? Good old England!' he thought, 'Jolly old front doors wide upon, and bells coming away in your hand!' He hesitated. Then he took the little parcel out of his pocket and stepped gingerly inside, it was a polite sort of movement, such as the Englishman makes when he is anxious to do a good turn, but on no account wants to be mistaken for an intruder, that would be dreadful. There wasn't a soul about. He saw a door, and decided to give a little knock.

This he did, gingerly.

'Come in,' a feminine voice said placidly.

Mr Bowling felt very intrusive, and was nervous in case he should be thought impertinent, and in case he should frighten the lady, whoever she was.

He opened the door, mouth and brain shaped to say instantly and politely: 'I say, I'm most frightfully sorry, and all that sort of thing? I couldn't make anyone hear, and I want to leave something for a Miss Mason?'

Then something very suddenly and swiftly happened to him: or, not to him, Bowling—but to the soul within him, and the Bowling who had been born a thousand thousand years before, telling him in a flash to prepare himself to receive the shocking knowledge, that, with God, all things were possible, and all things were in His Good Time.

The first thing his eyes settled on in the room was a crucifix standing between two candles.

And the second thing, a woman sitting by a coal fire, sewing.

Although she was ugly, he knew instantly that he had dragged his weary footsteps to the top of a very long and very steep hill. He had known her before, in some other day; or he had not known her ever before. It didn't really matter which. This was the woman he loved. Instantly his brain knew the very first great panic of his life. He realised, to the terrible depths, his great and awful mistake: he had been impatient, seeking to make his own time; whereas, the sordid world here belonged to God's Good Time. Too late, too late, a frightened whisper touched his brain, which had begun to burn like a fever. On the wall, it said: 'Whosoever shall seek to save his life—shall lose it'; and, of course, conversely was also the case. He felt a hundred years old, and he stood looking down at her in fear.

She seemed very placid. She wasn't a bit frightened, and she said she was Miss Mason. Her voice wasn't pretty, but it had a quality which excited the senses of Mr Bowling by the depths of kindness and understanding there. It was a lonely voice, and yet a contented voice in a spiritual sense. He stood like a small boy in front of her; fascinated. His brain-voice told him: 'You never thought falling in love would be like this, did you, Bowling! Yet how positive is all the world that love comes in just a single flash, like the stroke of a knife—it was born before, you see!' And cynical laughter flooded his nerves.

His voice had gone dry.

He stood holding his brown felt hat. His brain was already clearing, and the matter of love had slipped down to its proper place—the heart. He could feel it thumping.

Increasingly frightened, his drugged brain thought now:

'What have I done? Is it really too late?... What if Mr Clark enters the flat and finds ...? *That old idiot next door will probably tell him?*'

Beads of sweat broke out on Mr Bowling's forehead when it slowly came to him for the first time for a very long time indeed, *that he wanted to live;* he wanted to save himself.

'My God,' he thought in fright, 'what a *fool* I've been!'

It was queer, he thought later, that he didn't then think nearly completely enough: what made him flatter himself that Miss Mason would marry him? He knew she loved him, the knowledge had been given him as a gift when he entered the room: but what made him think she could marry him? He who was evil itself?

He only knew then that he wanted to save himself. He might save himself yet?

But he couldn't leave. She asked him to sit down, and he sat, hat on knee, thinking: 'Mr Clark is now entering the flat.

He is now stumbling over the body on the floor. He is now seeing the broken glasses. He is now, white-faced, telephoning the police.'

Miss Mason was saying about Mrs Nandle.

'How kind of her to remember my birthday. I'm thirty-four,' she said quaintly. She hardly ever looked up at Mr Bowling, it was rather as if she knew she was no beauty, and would prefer that her sewing enjoyed her countenance. She said she had heard about the death of Delius Nandle, and she said she was sorry.

'I'm very sorry too,' said Mr Bowling in a dry, subdued voice. He kept licking his lips. He was quite tongue-tied. A lover indeed! 'I dunno, I'm sure,' he kept thinking stupidly. 'Life tricks you at every bally turn!'

Miss Mason said lots of things. Her manner of saying things was rather motherly, it was positive, a little as if Mr Bowling was her son, and she wanted to give him bits of news before packing him off to school. Her father, she said, was vicar of a little village on the south coast, and she only came up here now and again to stay with his sister, who ran this place. She didn't say what 'this place' was, or where the sister was, or why the front door was wide open, or why the bell had come away in his hand. But she said that she didn't stay here for long as a rule. 'If anything upsets me,' she said, 'I go back to father.'

'Upsets you?' Mr Bowling heard himself say. He suddenly recognised the fact that, had he not gone down to the Nandles, he would never have met Miss Mason at all. And he recognised: 'And I only went down at all because I knew darned well I wanted to murder old Nandle—so what can you make of that?'

'When I say upset,' Miss Mason's ugly but kindly voice said, 'I suppose I mean I'm rather sensitive! My aunt gets cross,' was the only explanation she gave. 'She suffers a lot with gout.'

'Too much port,' wondered Mr Bowling stupidly. He wasn't really wanting to think that at all, it was just one of those many,

many thoughts which filtered into the brainbox like dirty ink into blotting paper.

'I love my father! He's quite alone, except for the old maid. I only come up here because he begs me to. I like being with him and the sea.'

'The sea,' said drugged Mr Bowling.

'I don't know what I shall do when he dies! He's ninety now,' she looked up for a second and smiled. She said she had never expected to marry, and Mr Bowling thought:

'Men are quite crazy! They think love must necessarily mean beauty of body! . . . But what does it matter about an ugly body? It's the soul . . .' He thought too: 'The soul is the mind, of course.'

Miss Mason said she was fond of Woolworths, but otherwise she didn't like London much. She liked Chelsea and the river there, if she found herself there, and Battersea Park.

Mr Bowling developed a passionate wish to get out in the street where there was air.

'I must think about this,' he thought frantically. 'For the Lord's sake let me out of here—I want to think!'

Miss Mason thanked him for coming, and when he got out in a dry voice that he thought he would like to come again, 'if I'm . . . free to,' both of them knew that he meant it, though neither knew if he would.

'Do please come whenever you like?' asked Miss Mason. 'Just come in, if the maid is out?'

He got out into the street and started walking feverishly in the wrong direction.

After a few moments of this, his terrible danger came back to him.

'Struth,' he thought frantically, 'I don't know what's the matter with me—I've got to get rid of that body!'

He started yelling in the street for a taxi, but there wasn't one, so he started running.

'If it isn't too late,' his feet tapped out. '*If it isn't too late?*'

His running feet tapped out awed prayers.

'Oh, God, what have I done? What have I done? What dreadful thing happened to me?

'Only grant me this,' he prayed, 'to get rid of the body, then I might have a sporting chance!'

He still didn't think about Miss Mason's point of view. Such was the vanity of man, and the overpowering confidence of love.

CHAPTER XIX

The solemn brightness of Miss Mason's green-grey eyes stayed with him as he ran. They looked alarmed and sad and full of knowledge. They looked young in the love-sense. They weren't thirty-four years old.

They hadn't seen a man's body; long lashes would flash down, guarding them from such a sight.

He streaked up the road like a rabbit.

He paused outside the Heights, getting his breath back, and preparing himself for either shock or relief. In the yellow gleam of light from the blacked-out swing doors, he looked like a stoat. He had died a thousand deaths; he had been caught by a dog, shot by a gun, beaten by a stick.

But he was here, and there was still a chance. He would know in a minute or two.

He went in very quickly and went straight to the lifts. They were both engaged, and he waited in dreadful suspense. The late Mr Farthing's shop looked silent and sinister and dark. Doubtless, down in the club, Daphne was beginning to wonder where he had got to.

The lift came at last and he got in alone and went up to the fifth floor. Here he opened the gates cautiously and quietly and peeped out.

He took a frightful shock and plunged forward with a cry. Old Cooker and the manager were at his door; Mr Clark was extending a key.

'Ah, there you are,' apologised Mr Clark, withdrawing the key.

Mr Bowling let out a gasp. He scurried forward, a strange, plunging movement.

'Can't ask you in,' he gasped, pale. 'Frightfully sorry, but . . .' He broke off, panting, the two men staring at him.

Whenever this sort of thing happened to Mr Clark at the Heights, it was not a surprise, it meant there was a woman in hiding. He always tapped the side of his long nose and squinted slightly, and pursed his lips slightly, and nudged whoever was nearest.

'Ah,' he always nudged, 'I see!' and he said something about being men of the world. After all, they had to keep the flats full, it was all very well to think about morals, rents were the thing to think about.

Mr Clark laughed, and Mr Bowling managed to laugh.

Mr Cooker, frustrated again, stared stupidly at the two of them. What was the manager nudging him for? What? Oh— woman? Oh . . . ! Mr Cooker had forgotten all about women, it was ages since he'd gone in for that lark.

'It was just that Mr Cooker thought he heard a burglar in your flat, Mr Bowling!'

Mr Bowling stood with his back to the flat door, smiling.

'I know, old man! He told me! But it was nonsense,' he laughed.

Mr Clark laughed. His great nose was inclined to be bulbous. He ended his laugh with it.

'And the only other thing was, Mr Bowling, I understood that you were leaving? Or so I thought? But the cleaner is a Belgian, and she must have misunderstood.'

'I'm staying,' said Mr Bowling. 'So far as I know.'

'Well, that is splendid,' said Mr Clark, and began to move off.

'Splendid?' Mr Bowling's smiling voice said.

'Splendid?' queried Mr Cooker, disappointed. It had all fallen very flat. All the excitement, and now nothing at all, and Bowling not even going to ask him in for a drink? But he couldn't, could he, if he'd got a woman in there? *Had* he got a woman in there?

Mr Cooker jolly well knew he had not. He thought: 'Shall I stop up a bit longer? Might hear something further? Or shall I go to bed?'

Mr Bowling, slipping quickly into his flat, was thinking;

'Safe—so far;' and he was thinking what he would do with

the late Mr Farthing. 'It will be a very risky journey indeed,' he thought, 'but a little later on I'll try and get him down to his furniture shop, and bung him in there. Can't have him up here, when the Belgian turns up in the morning!'

He switched on the bedroom light. The late Mr Farthing surprised him very much by already showing signs of getting stiff. 'Rigor mortis,' he thought. Mr Farthing was lying face downwards, and his nose had bled on the carpet.

'It looks as if I'd better not delay things,' thought Mr Bowling.

With a resolute expression, he first of all tidied up the flat, collecting the broken glass and wrapping it in newspapers and putting it in the kitchen.

He glanced at his watch. It was gone ten to eleven, and the club shut at eleven. He had it in mind to slip down and see if Daphne had taken fright yet, over Farthing's prolonged absence. Farthing had never missed an evening in the club, it was one of the accepted facts about the place that 'old Farthing's on his stool as usual, shooting off his ugly mouth!' First, he must spend a very gloomy few minutes washing up the blood, it was on Farthing's ugly mouth, and had dried all over his broad nose, and it was on his hands, backs and fronts. Mr Bowling went and got his flannel and some hot water and a basin and some soap. He returned with it to the bedroom. When he had completed this singularly unpleasant task to his satisfaction, and brushed Mr Farthing's clammy hair, he proceeded to pare Mr Farthing's nails. They were sure to be full of bits of his murderer's skin, or clothes, and would betray him under the microscope. Mr Farthing's frightened eyes were wide open the whole time, watching him, and looking as if it was rather painful, having your nails carefully pared after you were dead. When he had finished, Mr Bowling shoved Mr Farthing's dead head to and fro, rather fascinated by his broken neck, you could get it back an incredibly long way. Then he lugged Mr Farthing up and shoved him into the low chair in the bedroom, by the dressing table. He wanted to test his weight,

and to see how he sagged. He sagged very badly when he tried
to hold him upright, his toes hanging down, and his great head
flopping forward. Mr Bowling got his own brown felt hat and
shoved it on Mr Farthing's head. It was a little too big, and Mr
Farthing looked extremely grotesque in the deep chair there, with
his knees all cock-eyed, and his shoulders sagging forward, and
the brown hat bent in prayer. Mr Bowling looked at his watch
again and hurried out.

On the way down, he noticed very carefully indeed every
step of the way, counting the paces and the number of stairs—
he dared not use the lift—and wondering, when he got to the
ground floor, if he really dare take the frightful risk of crossing
the corner of the entrance lounge, along to the merciful shadows
in front of Farthing's shop?

'I've simply got to,' he thought. 'There are no two ways about
it! I'll bung him in his bally shop, turn the place upside down,
and who's to say I'm the one who beat him up?'

He hurried into the club.

Daphne had the club almost to herself.

'Where's everybody tonight?' he remarked, sitting at the
counter and smiling at her.

Daphne was wearing her kilt. He ordered an Advocat, and
offered her one, which she accepted.

'Thanks, I will!'

'I suppose all the world is firewatching,' he commented.

'I think there's a binge on somewhere,' she told him. 'There
are a few in the billiard room, though. There's a match on.'

She didn't say a word about Farthing.

'Well, cheerio, my dear,' he said.

'Cheers,' she said, and pursed her lips like a spout.

'You're looking very well, Daphne.'

'Good,' she beamed.

He kept saying things, not wanting to ask direct where
Farthing was. He'd better be careful.

'Haven't seen you lately,' she said.

'No.'

'Been away?'

'Yes . . .'

'Country?'

'Yes,' he said, but didn't enlarge.

'I like the country,' she said, 'now and again. I wouldn't like to live there, though.'

'I dunno,' he said. 'I'm a bit browned off with town. I don't think I'd mind clearing out. For a time, anyhow.'

'I hate the sea,' she leaned on the counter and said.

'Oh, I like the sea,' he said.

Conversation dried. He asked for another Advocat, and lit a fag. He went to the money machine.

But he lost everything he put in, continually getting almost three nines, and almost three fives, but never quite.

'I hope my luck isn't run out,' he said nervously.

Her laugh came.

'Keep trying,' she said.

'Have you cut your head?' she said.

He started.

He also thought: 'Miss Mason must have noticed my head? She never said a word, and she never looked at it! There's breeding, for you!'

'Fell,' he said, at the money machine.

'Tight again,' she sing-songed, and started doctoring up her square face in a tiny mirror. She was like a cat, licking at things, and dabbing at herself, and preening. She'd purr in a minute, he thought.

'Oh, well,' he yawned, and sat on Mr Farthing's stool, one hand holding his fag and the liqueur glass, the other in his pocket, 'Ah,' he said, unable to stand the strain any longer, 'but I'm sitting on Mr Farthing's stool! Mustn't do that!' He got up and finished his liqueur, glancing at her out of the corners of his eyes.

'That's all right,' she said, powdering. 'He won't mind! What if he does?'

Nervous and irritated, he looked in the billiard room. But he didn't want to be dragged into some conviviality or other, and withdrew again. The cues were going: 'Cli'k ... cli'k ...' Admiral Leopard was behind a big cigar, tugging for the chalk.

'Goodnight, Daphne,' Mr Bowling said.

'Cheerio, dear,' she said, and smiled and started washing glasses. 'Time, gentlemen, please,' she sing-songed, forgetting him completely. 'It's eleven,' her voice followed him.

He went up in the lift.

'Hell,' he thought. He thought: 'Anyhow, she doesn't appear to be worried about him!'

He went into his flat.

. . . The worst of being an amateur at crime, and particularly murder he reflected with considerable anxiety, was that you hadn't spent a lifetime studying the tricks of the trade. You'd never even pinched anything. It had been very different in the recent days when you wanted to be caught; but, now, when you would almost sell your soul for life and liberty and new-found love, the most terrible crisis threatened second by second: any second, you might make a fatal slip; the thread would break, down would come the sword of Damocles, and a sorry visit to old Charybdis. Mr Bowling knew that his heart was beating, and that he was very much afraid. And when he was really afraid, his nervousness betrayed itself by an attitude of nonchalance, and rather tuneless whistling. He whistled *Hot Sock Roleson* and proceeded to put on his bowler hat. He went into his bedroom where the late Mr Farthing was still sitting looking dejected, felt hat bent downwards. The late Mr Farthing's left arm had slipped downwards in a hanging position gloomy to behold. 'The fellow weighs a ton,' murmured Mr Bowling. 'I shall be damn lucky if I get away with this! What do I do—drag him?' He bent and put his arms about Mr Farthing, and heaved him up and out into the little hall. Everything about Mr Farthing hung heavily downwards in a thoroughly unhelpful manner, and the felt hat fell off. Mr Bowling dropped him and put the hat back on again. 'If only you knew it,' he murmured nervously, 'you are looking extremely silly!' On an impulse, he opened the front door and peeped out. There was nobody about, 'No,' he thought, 'but the moment I ruddy well start my act, the bally passage will be alive with people!' He went back.

He tried a little rehearsal in the flat. He got an arm round Mr Farthing, hoisted him up, and took him for a little walk up and down the sitting room. Mr Farthing didn't like it at all. He hung back shyly, and sloped downwards modestly, and the hat fell off again. Mr Bowling dropped him in disgust and sat in the armchair and lit a fag. He sat smoking and staring at him. 'I shall never do it,' he feared. 'I shall never make it in a thousand years!' He sat smoking and staring. He wondered whether to lump him out of the window. No, no! They'd easily trace him back to this flat. Some bally technical thing would give the show away. Measurements! And to dump him out in the passage and go to bed was equally silly. And just the same risk. 'I've got to do it,' he decided. 'First thoughts are best! I've got to get him down to his shop!'

He had an idea and got up again, stubbing out his cigarette. He went into the bedroom and got a dark coloured silk handkerchief. It was those dragging legs of Farthing's. 'I was jolly good at the three legged race at school,' he remembered. 'Opposite legs tied together, arms intertwined.'

The late Mr Farthing did not at all like intertwining his arm with Mr Bowling, and he made a considerable fuss about it, looking resentful, with the felt hat crushed down over his eyes, and the left side of his body tied by the leg to Mr Bowling's right. Mr Bowling finally managed to put the dead left arm into his own pocket.

'Now,' said Mr Bowling.

Mr Cooker was putting on a pair of red-striped pyjamas. He was tired of thinking he heard guns, or of thinking that fellow Bowling had got somebody in there. He twice went to his door and softly opened it; but the first time he found that it was Miss Phelps opposite who had opened a door, so as to put out a milk bottle. She would do the dustbin next, like she always did, last thing. So when he again heard a door open, Mr Cooker did not go to the door, feeling sure it was Miss Phelps again with her dustbin.

Now, quietly, he again thought he heard a door open, was it hers or Mr Bowling's?

There was a distinct sound of somebody passing his door.

It was from Mr Bowling's direction.

Mr Cooker did not care to go to the door with his pyjamas undone, and without his dressing gown, just in case Miss Phelps might see him, for that would be most improper. So he hurriedly tied up his pyjamas and flung on his dressing gown.

He went to his door and softly opened it.

Just too late.

He saw a shadow disappear round the corner to the lifts, rather a bulky shadow.

'Damn,' said Mr Cooker.

'Damn,' said Mr Bowling, and was forced to take a rest. He was no weakling, but this was terrific. He got Farthing up against a corner of the stairs, thank goodness the lights were so delightfully dim on the stairs, what excellent economy! People rarely used the stairs, unless the lifts were broken down; if somebody passed now, and saw the two of them, a bowler hat and a felt hat, they might reasonably think of drunks, especially if one had the breath to whistle. Mr Bowling started to whistle, but heard approaching footsteps. All the moisture went out of his mouth and his whistling ceased. He stood stock still, heart thumping.

The footsteps took a turn away, and faded out.

'Come along,' murmured Mr Bowling. 'You'll get me hanged, if we hang about here! Please remember—I can't drop you and bolt for it! Our legs are tied together!'

He got his burden safely down to the last flight. Increasing light at his feet indicated the curtained entrance from the staircase to the foyer.

Twenty yards, now; but a sheer gauntlet of light, and possibly porters and people.

There was the drone of voices, and the sound of somebody using the stamp machine.

He waited.

'No,' a girl's voice said.

'What for?' a man's voice said.

'Well, I've written, anyway! Shall I post it here, darling?'

'Better post it outside!'

'We can post it here!'

'You do whatever you think,' the man's voice said.

'Shall I? Or shan't I?'

'Make up your mind,' Mr Bowling said, through his teeth. 'My arm's nearly breaking!'

CHAPTER XX

HE counted: one, two, three, four, five—six.

He went through the curtains. Straining every muscle in his body, he got Mr Farthing out into the brilliant light of the foyer. There was a man reading a novel by the fire there. He didn't look up, and Mr Bowling safely reached the shop, and the shadowed angle where was the door. As he did so, out of the corner of his eyes he saw a police inspector and a sergeant enter the foyer holding torches.

They were doing the rounds, looking for lights from improperly blacked-out windows. To do this, they had to pass close to the shop front, and out into the inner yard where the bicycles were stacked. Mr Bowling thought:

'I've got about four seconds before they reach me,' and at the same moment realised it had not occurred to him that the shop door would naturally be locked. His shaking hand tried the handle, and it didn't budge.

He held Farthing tightly against the glass door and offered up a prayer. With his free hand he frantically started groping in Mr Farthing's pockets for the key. It must obviously be on him. He found it on him, it was in his left hand trouser pocket—but it was on a chain and it didn't reach the door. The two voices drew nearer and nearer.

Nearer and nearer.

An angular light from one of their torches showed Mr Bowling the picture of his face, and the late Mr Farthing's face, flattened against the glass of the shop door.

Frozen with fear, he could only stand there, flat, waiting.

Time ceased altogether.

*

The officers of the law, however, heard the small, faraway voice of Destiny say:

'Look over *this* way! Really, the way those Smiths do their windows is a disgrace, their light can be seen down by the river!'

They vanished.

Mr Bowling got the key off the chain, got the door open and fell in.

He softly closed the door again and locked it. He sat on the floor, all but collapsed, and started to undo the silk handkerchief round his leg. 'Now is not the time to collapse,' he thought. 'While I am in here, there is constant danger!'

He put the handkerchief in his pocket, resolved to forget nothing. He took out a pair of gloves from his pocket, and carefully put them on. He may be an amateur, but he had read all about finger prints. He dragged Mr Farthing along the floor a bit until he bumped into something. Nervously, he struck a match, instantly blowing it out again. It was all right, the blackout arrangements were done for the night, and in any case he had seen inside the shop enough to know the geography of the place fairly well. He went into Mr Farthing's little office, closing the door and finding the lamp switch. Quietly but thoroughly, he turned the place upside down, contents of the drawers on the floor, ledgers on the floor, everything on the floor. Then he put out the light and returned to the shop.

But Mr Bowling had not remembered the geography of the little shop quite so well as he had thought. Crossing as he thought, with utmost care to the door, he bumped ever so slightly into something, and to his horrified ears there proceeded to come a series of resounding crashes of shattered china horses and plates.

It was immediately followed by a rattling on the door.

He stood stock still in the darkness.

With great presence of mind, as he thought, Mr Bowling was remembering Mr Farthing's key, when the voice called.

'Mr Farthing? Is that you . . . ? Who's there?'

It was Daphne.

'Who's there, I say? Mr Farthing . . . ?'

He had got the key back on the chain when her step moved away. He knew very well that he had about a split-second chance of getting out unseen. 'My gloves,' he thought, fairly calmly, and groped about. He had been obliged to take them off in order to get the key back on the ring. He groped about, telling his trembling body: 'Steady, now, don't panic whatever you do! Or you'll make a mess of it!' He got his gloves, put them on as he groped his way like a blind man to the door. There must be no finger prints on the door knob.

He found the door knob, opened it slowly and cautiously— and slipped out. He closed it and in a third of a second was in safety.

As he re-entered the foyer, Daphne came round the corner by the stamp machine, with Mr Clark. Neither looked at him and he went quietly up the stairs.

When he reached his flat he went straight to the bathroom and was violently sick. Afterwards, he took off all his clothes and wrapped them in a parcel. They had blood on them, and some of the blood might be Mr Farthing's. He put the parcel in the kitchen cupboard which was under the sink, until such time as he had decided what to do with it. He was going to do something with it that very night, the sooner the better. Then he had a bath and dressed again. He could honestly say that he felt as safe as anybody else in the entire block of flats, for the late Mr Farthing had had many enemies. He felt refreshed and rather admired himself in his blue suit. He had a brandy in the sitting room, knowing what he was now going to do; he was going to write a very long letter. The bruise on his temple was a bit sore, and might be rather telltale; but somehow or other he felt optimistic and confident and clear headed. He didn't feel at all like sleep.

'Coffee,' he suddenly thought. It would be very nice to have a lot of sweet, black coffee.

'It will help me to write,' he thought.

And while the coffee was brewing, he stood with his hands deep in his trousers pockets, and burst out laughing.

'B'rf!' he burst. 'Good Lor', what a bally scare—what?' He thought: 'Phew!' He went in for quite a lot of little laughs.

Then, he sat before the white sheets of paper, his brow furrowed, and his face saddened, rather as if he was a man about to write out a plea which he knew jolly well could never succeed. Yet, he must write it.

'My last and only chance,' he thought, 'of happiness!'

He put those actual words, too. His last and only chance of happiness, but adding humbly that he knew how very slight that chance was, 'and little I deserve to come to it.'

He started the letter in quite the ordinary manner, putting 'My dear Miss Mason', after all, he didn't know her very well. He explained that it was all very well to say he had known her all his life, ever since she was a little girl over a school fence, whom he'd called Angel; but that seemed rather silly, now. In matters of etiquette, he had only met Miss Mason once, and despite the depth of his feelings, he could not even go so far as to ask her christian name.

In the same humble way, he signed the letter: 'Yours sincerely, W. Bowling'. In the rather sacred atmosphere of thought and feeling, under the deeply human and spiritual strain of which he wrote, it seemed rather dreadful to write a common-or-garden name like William; and as for its distressing abbreviation—Bill— well, it was not to be thought of, it was like forgetting oneself and exclaiming 'Gosh' in church. He said to Miss Mason that he had sinned 'most inordinately, and in a more serious way than other men,' and while he did not seek to excuse it, for that would rob from the voluntary act of penitence, which, although he was not a Roman Catholic, was such an integral part of his feelings and beliefs, he did yet feel 'that I have come to the end of a very long and very dark journey, on foot, and much of the journey was through a wood, where there were one or two bears to kill.' He said when he walked into her room, and saw the crucifix standing there in between the two candles, 'I felt I had come home. And you were sitting there, and there was everything about you, and about your room, which helped me to understand.'

Then he told her in detail all about his murders.

Also he said:

'Which brings me to the very great question as to whether we are to believe that punishment for sin is of necessity meted out in this world; or held over. In the battle for Good and Evil, which takes place in all of us, surely that battle can hardly be said to have come to the last round until Death? . . . Yet, how fully I know that I am now merely praying and seeking and hoping for two things: that God will reserve Judgment on me for a time—and that you will believe my penitence and sincerity, and succeed in understanding my motive, for, I dare to say, motive is everything in all things? How often do we hear said—it was the thought behind it? For my part, if the head is full of penitence for wrongs done, and the heart full of Heaven-sent love, and the soul full of good music, there you have the man, and such a man can reasonably plead: I have made a mess of things, through fog and impatience—pity me.'

When Mr Bowling stopped and re-read passages like that, he felt himself going rather red. 'Struth,' he thought shyly. 'Hark at me!' But he meant it all, and was secretly rather pleased with his writing, thinking modestly: 'H'm—yes, that's pretty good, what? I rather like that.'

Here and there through the letter, he made it sound as if he and Miss Mason were here together, talking. 'Believe me, Miss Mason, I am trying so hard to convince you.'

And:

'Well, Miss Mason, I can only assure you that, even as I write this very long letter to you, my mood alternates minute by minute. One minute I think I may yet have the very great good fortune of hearing from you that my plea is not in vain; and the next—that when I call for your answer I shall find only your empty room, yourself and the crucifix gone, like a dear but sorry dream. You will have gone back, upset, to your father.'

He concluded with rather a nice bit about 'the kindly silence of the night, I am sitting here alone, and yet in the knowledge that, whatever your answer, I can never really be alone again. Please believe in my sincerity, Miss Mason?'

CHAPTER XXI

HE fell asleep at the table.

He slept there, waking into semi-consciousness now and again, but only to change his position and to rest his chin on the other arm.

When he finally woke up properly it was three in the morning. He walked about, yawning, had a wash and made himself a cup of tea.

Then he walked about, sipping from the cup, and holding the letter he had written, reading over paragraphs and feeling pleased and hopeful.

'How wonderful could the future be . . . If only a man knew that patience and complete blindness was the right thing always, and trust in Destiny . . . Never to try and force things . . . The dreadful need, which is not a need at all, to inflict suffering on others.

'How guilty I have been, Miss Mason. I wonder if you like Wordsworth, I have been sitting reading *Guilt and Sorrow.* Afterwards my eyes fell on *Troilus and Cressida,* which appealed to my present mood much more—but I cannot wait ten days for my Cressid, either. Yet well may I have to. You must be bound to fly from me, in horror.'

This passage was a subtle signal for a sense of gloom. It came to him, as he licked the flap of the envelope, that his cause was utterly hopeless.

Shall I even send it her, he wondered; yet sat writing her name even as he spoke aloud. Miss Mason, 66 Brook Green, London, W6.

He watched it dry, deciding, 'I'll go out now, and pop it in her letter-box myself.'

He went and got the parcel from under the sink.

He walked slowly, still half undecided about the whole thing. He was not afraid of the consequences, were she to hand his letter straight to the police; it was not that. It was deeper than that. He was merely afraid that, in her judgment of him, she might decide it was also his punishment to die alone, without the consolation of seeing her once again, and savouring the aura which surrounded her, an aura which could be likened only to spiritual Lilies of the Valley. It was as if God lowered her down on a long string every so often; her face was naturally a bit frozen and pinched, and her nose a bit red, it was so cold up there: but you got a whiff of her, and you knew at once where she had come from. You thought:

'Lilies of the Valley! How wonderful!' And you wanted to stop with her for always.

. . . Nobody stopped him when he walked out of the Heights, whistling *Hot Sock Roleson.* The night porter was sunk into the lounge sofa, his white head thrown back in abandon, legs and arms outstretched like a dropped puppet, and his mouth wide open. Mr Bowling did not look in the direction of the late Mr Farthing's shop, and he did not allow himself to think: 'I wonder I have not had visitors before this; one would imagine a flat to flat visit, surely? Or at least detectives at the entrance here?' He felt just a little unnerved, as he passed through the curtains. It would have been inconvenient to have been stopped and asked: ''Ere, you—where'd you think you're going? What's in that parcel?' It would be awful to be stopped before he had got the note to Miss Mason, even though he was not sure he was going to deliver it to Miss Mason. In the same way, it did matter about being found with the suit, and it didn't. One couldn't tell yet. He just had it in mind to get rid of it, whereas, in another mood, he wouldn't have bothered at all. And, by the way, where to put it? . . . It had not occurred to him that, vast though London is, its eyes are vaster, and there simply is nowhere you can shove a suit which has blood on it, short of a furnace, but Mr Bowling hadn't got a furnace.

When he reached Miss Mason's, the suit was still under his arm.

Dawn was just beginning to shove out sleepy grey arms, and to push a slightly pink face from beneath the blankets. It yawned and its misty breath was blackish and chilly. Then a distinctly red nose sat bolt upright over Hammersmith way.

Mr Bowling, after many hesitations, found the letter box, took a very deep breath and popped his letter in. He was just thinking: 'Well, I've done it now, that's that,' and regretting that he had forgotten to put *By Hand* in the top left hand corner, in the way he had been brought up to do, when he was considerably astonished to hear a footstep behind him.

'God morning,' said Miss Mason in very matter-of-fact tones.

He was astounded.

Speechless with shyness, it was only after several seconds of staring eagerly at her, that he remembered that there was a war on.

Miss Mason, getting out her latch key, was saying that she had been on part time duty at a shelter, not saying which shelter, or what she had been on duty for, thereby leaving him to choose between the Red Cross or the St John's Ambulance Brigade, for he was perfectly sure that she was an administering angel of some kind.

He felt extremely foolish, being caught at such an hour, and heard himself mumbling apologies. He said, no, he would not dream of coming in at such an hour, it would be most inconvenient, he knew, and might be thought improper were anyone to observe them.

'I am thinking of you,' he said, longing to come in, as a tramp longs for warmth and sanctuary, but staying firmly on the doorstep.

Miss Mason explained that the girls lived their own lives here entirely, and were free to come and go, or to have men visitors to meals in their room, any old thing like that. She was bright and sounded so nice. She didn't look too bad in the morning light. She had a hat which rather tended to shoot upwards in a peculiar way, but he thought, on the whole, hats suited her. She had given him a small hand which was a bit chapped. It felt as if somebody had put into his fist a sugar mouse, like the things one used to eat as kids.

He heard himself saying that he had only tootled along to leave a note for her, 'though, you may think it odd of me, Miss Mason,' he faltered.

She said at once:

'No, I don't, why should I?' and it sounded as if she had been expecting him to come at that very hour.

'How nice of you to say that,' he said.

'I would like it if you would come in?' she said. 'Won't you?'

He said, no, he really wouldn't, but he found himself standing once again in her little room where the crucifix was, and he heard himself saying: 'No, I won't sit down, this is too bad of me' even as he sat on the sofa and put his parcel beside him.

She hadn't said a word more about his note, and had been far too tactful to go and hoik it out of the letter-box, what breeding was there, eh? The room was pleasantly fuggy from the night before, and the fire was not quite out. It smelt of burnt wood. Miss Mason put on one light and sat opposite him in her usual chair. He felt as if they two could simply sit there, not saying anything, for a million years. It was queer. It was natural. He no longer said: 'Am I balmy?'

It seemed perfectly natural, after a little while, to be discussing love and marriage with her, and how things which happened suddenly and crazily were always 'right.' Other people wouldn't believe it, if you told them. They'd giggle, embarrassed, wanting to believe you, and half believing you, but crying: 'Oh—nuts! Hark at you!'

'It's what makes life so interesting,' was one remark Miss Mason made.

Another remark she made was that she thought love was all-forgiving, if it was the right kind of love.

'There,' feared Mr Bowling, 'I don't think I can agree with you. But not because I don't want to, God knows!'

'Well, it is so with me.'

'There might be some things,' he suggested, 'which are too serious for mortal consideration. I can't see even you forgiving everything, Miss Mason. I wish I could.'

'Such as?' she asked quietly.

But he dared not say.

'I just wanted to write you,' he said. 'And I awfully wanted to see you just once more. I'm very lucky.'

'It's I who am lucky,' she said.

They sat quietly, and he knew quite well that she loved him, and had as good as accepted him—except for the dreadful snag which she did not yet know. How can she marry me, he told himself, once she has read my letter? It was all very well to theorise about forgiving a man everything. Yes, everything but that one thing.

'I must not keep you any longer,' he said, and stood up. He forgot his parcel, but neither noticed it.

She stood up.

'Shall I see you again?' she said.

'I wonder,' he said quietly, and turned away. He was afraid to take her hand. He ought not to touch her.

She was saying that she hadn't expected love.

'I'm grateful,' she murmured, not to him, but to the crucifix, and he had the idea she would be praying soon after he had gone.

When he said goodbye, it was as if he knew he would never see her again. But she said:

'I'm not going to say goodbye.' And he was again uplifted.

'Aren't you?'

'No . . .'

'You must read my letter, before you decide anything.' He smiled: 'I'm so afraid that when I call again—you will be gone?'

*

Again, he thought:

'She won't be gone . . . ! I believe she knows now . . . ! she understands now . . . !'

Breathlessly, his heart started to sing, with the waking birds. He walked a long way, as far as the river, and then back, arriving back at the Heights feeling inwardly crowded with joy and hope, and striding out of the lift on the fifth floor and with springy step going to his flat door.

Where he stopped dead.

Like an icy hand, something touched his heart, and he felt his blood go chilly.

Two men stood there, at his door; but it wasn't so much at them that he looked, as at the thing held in the hand of one of them: a brown felt hat.

His pending doom took the shape of a tottering house in his brain. The world had been getting so right, it had seemed; but the world was made of cards: and even as it fell a straight-looking man walked forward holding handcuffs, and saying: 'Mr Bowling, is it? I'm Chief Inspector Smart, from Scotland Yard. This is Detective Inspector Chase.' And they both said in frightful chorus:

'Is this your hat?'

. . . Mr Bowling told himself that he had not gone pale, and that if ever his public school manner could be an advantage, that time was surely now.

He must act as he had never acted in his life before.

'By jove,' he said sleekly, 'hat? By jove, but it looks like it, old man, let's have a look . . . ! But I'm forgetting my manners, won't you come in?'

'We will,' commented Chief Inspector Smart in rather sepulchral tones.

Mr Bowling decided it was best not to whistle *Hot Sock Roleson*, in case it should be construed as overacting. Cards must now be played with the very greatest care. Every sentence he allowed himself to make, must have that wealth of pre-thought which time and conditions made possible.

'Well, now,' he said sombrely, having led the way to the sitting room. 'Let's have a look at it, what?'

'Biffed your head,' wondered the Chief Inspector, and Mr Bowling, affecting to be startled, said, what, oh, that, yes, nasty tumble, bally blackout—and gave a bit of a laugh. 'Been out?' was another thing Smart rather wondered, glancing at his watch.

Mr Bowling said it was a bit early, but he had a lifelong habit of walking in the early mornings, if it wasn't too wet, and he'd been down by the river.

He stood holding the brown hat and saying, yes, it was his, he was sure. He tried it on and it fitted him perfectly. They'd wanted to put his name in it, at the shop, but he'd not waited.

'I know,' Smart said.

'Ah,' said Mr Bowling.

'Henry Heath. We got the chap out of bed.'

'Ah . . . !'

'Lucky he had your address,' Smart stood ponderously in the room and said. Detective Chase stared like a ferret.

Nobody had mentioned murder yet, so Mr Bowling decided it would be in order to give a puzzled little laugh and say:

'Well, now, I'm afraid I'm a bit in the dark, don't you know? What is all this in aid of?'

'You haven't asked us where we found the hat,' Smart said in a certain way. He gave a kind of glint at Chase.

'Nor he has,' said Chase.

'Nor I have,' said Mr Bowling, at just the right speed and tempo. 'I'm waiting all ears for you to tell me.'

The Belgian's latchkey was heard in the door just as they told him.

'Struth,' said Mr Bowling quite perfectly. 'You don't say so—bust his neck? How frightful?'

'H'm,' said Chief Inspector Smart. He didn't move from where he was, and went on to say he'd got a little job on, going round to all the flats, and there were nine hundred and three, finding out just where everyone was last night at, say, between ten and eleven.

'That's easy with me,' Mr Bowling said, cleverly he thought, 'I was right here! Or was I? Wait a minute . . . I know I had something to eat at the Coach and Horses in Notting Hill Gate, and then I went to see a . . . well, an acquaintance in Brook Green, Number Sixty-six, a Miss Mason. But as for exact times, I'm going to be perfectly honest and say I'm damn bad at them!'

'H'm! All the same,' Smart glinted at Chase ponderously, 'I think we'd better go carefully into them, Mr Bowling, don't you?'

Mr Bowling said, oh, rather, to be sure, it was whatever the Inspector said, he didn't know anything about routine matters. 'But won't you sit down?' he invited them both, becoming aware of a very unpleasant sound of the Belgian in the kitchen there, evidently examining the broken glasses from the night before, another item he had forgotten. 'Really,' he thought, 'I'm darn glad I've done with murder. If I get away with this, I shall take up something which doesn't need such a bally head for detail.' The Belgian kept rustling paper in there, and dropping bits of glass, and at any moment he expected her to come in and interrupt what the Inspector was now saying, which was that the late Mr Farthing seemed to have had quite a bit of a fight. 'But we don't think he was murdered there,' Smart said, using that very uncomfortable word for the first time. 'We think he was murdered some little time before he was put there.'

'Oh?' invited Mr Bowling gravely.

'And that fake burglary was a very sorry affair,' Smart said unflatteringly. 'A proper bungler, I should say!' But, Smart said, 'I don't propose to bore you with details, Mr Bowling . . . Not just now.'

'Ah . . . !'

'It's this time element,' Smart said. 'Since we can't seem to get it quite straight, I wonder if you'd mind coming down to the Yard with me? Were you doing anything very special today?'

Mr Bowling's mouth had gone rather dry. Before he could say that his time today could be devoted entirely to the Inspector, the Belgian came in.

He gave her a quick look, seeing what was in her hands.

But it was only his breakfast.

She layed it methodically as usual, showing not the slightest trace of surprise at seeing visitors, and leaving no indication whatever of what she had done with the broken glass.

'Door panel gone?' wondered Smart, next.

'. . . Yes . . .'

'But it's easy to put your foot through them, I'm sure?'

Then Smart said:

'Well, now, you'll be wanting your breakfast, Mr Bowling.'

But, as the two men looked like staying while he ate it, Mr Bowling said breezily:

'As a matter of fact I'm not a bit hungry.'

'Good,' said Smart at once. 'Then shall we get down to the Yard? I know they'll be very grateful indeed for your help down there?' And he led the way out.

The Belgian showed no surprise of any kind at all, and Mr Bowling was disconcerted to notice that Detective Chase remained behind.

'They're always very glad to give you a cup of tea at the Yard,' Chief Inspector Smart was saying interestingly. 'And maybe a sandwich, if the hanging about makes you peckish.'

Mr Bowling, having been expensively educated to believe life was one long and riotous road of excitement and opportunity, had never thought he would be expected to spend the whole of it in a small green room with bars to the window, and a sort of grating which suggested that others could peep in, but you could not peep out. As hour succeeded hour, and he sat on the hard chair, or paced up and down, or rang the bell and asked a policeman

for permission to send out for some more Gold Flake, his life
flashed before him, as it was said to flash before the drowning.
'And I am almost drowned,' he had decided long since. They
sent him in some stewed rabbit and carrots at one o'clock, and
invited him to send out for some beer. But he was past alcohol.
He was past food too, and didn't touch it for a little time, eating
it when it got cold only because he thought failure to do so might
be part of the test against him. With the sadism of the Japanese,
paper and pens in abundance was on the table there. But he
knew: 'I've made my confession—and I'm not making it again.
B'rf—I'm going to fight!' He stood with his hands deep in his
trouser pockets and knew: 'I'm in the toughest spot of my life!'
He also knew that to hang a man, you needed pretty good
evidence; and before you could even arrest him.

Well, there, God knew there must be plenty that their modern
methods could find.

They'd gone to Miss Mason's. That was to check up the
time. Smart had told him that soon after bringing him here.
Hours ago. Months, years ago.

The damn clock was striking three.

'I suppose they think I'll crack under this suspense,' thought
Mr Bowling.

Resolutely, he paced up and down whistling *Hot Sock Roleson*.

Not until four o'clock struck did the door open.

'Now for it,' thought Mr Bowling, and allowed himself to be
conducted upstairs and into a well-carpeted room with two men
and a roaring fire. He had just decided to indicate some reasonable and careful annoyance at being detained in this astounding
manner, and for the entire day, simply because he had probably
left his felt hat in the club one night, and Farthing had pinched
it, when he was compelled to give a very slight start. His eyes
fell on the nearest of the two men, who was about to leave the
room. It was Chief Inspector Thwaite, from Knockholt.

*

This was a bit of a jolt and he took in a breath. It was like when Mickey Mouse peeped cautiously at the trap and went: 'Ar—ar?' and stepped more gingerly and in the dark of the pantry.

Nor did Mr Bowling trust Thwaite's apparently genial manner, when he said:

'We've met before, I think? The unfortunate death of Delius Nandle . . .' and Mr Bowling noticed that he did not shake hands. He merely nodded, paused, and went out without speaking.

Mr Bowling turned to face a personality which he saw at once was not one to play bad cards with.

'Sit down, Mr Bowling,' the personality said suavely, and his hand moved slightly.

Tuning in, Mr Bowling thought. Whatever I say is being transcribed in the other room there.

'Thanks,' he said, sitting and crossing his legs easily, and making a point of not smoking. 'No, thanks,' he declined. He was not going to do anything which might indicate nervous stress.

The Superintendent thought:

'Funny how they all refuse to smoke up here, so as to prove they've nothing to feel nervous about!'

He sat back and smoked himself and said:

'I'm sorry to have kept you so long, Bowling. But the fact is we've become rather interested in you.' There was a pause.

Mr Bowling glanced at the other, sideways. He saw a very intelligent oval face, rather pink, and sleek grey hair brushed smartly back. The eyes were like deep river water in mid-winter.

'Typical copper,' he thought cynically. 'Why doesn't he get on with it?' His mood was turning black.

'Flattered, I'm sure,' he challenged, and then reined himself. He smiled. Silly to get annoyed . . .

The Superintendent was looking down at some papers.

'Here are all the replies you made to Inspector Smart this morning when you arrived.'

'Yes?'

'Miss Mason was interviewed this morning.'

'Ah . . . !'

'And,' said the other, 'she has signed a statement saying that you were with her from eight o'clock in the evening, until about twenty to eleven.' Mr Bowling's face gave a sudden very slight spasm. *What?*. . . 'We have checked up that you *could* therefore have reached the Heights Squash Club by ten minutes to eleven, as you stated!' He looked up. 'I perhaps ought to apologise to you, by the way, for keeping you, but you must appreciate that you were vague about the times, and said you were in your flat between ten and eleven!'

Mr Bowling grappled with his thoughts.

'Well, er . . .'

'We are all vague about something,' commented the Superintendent. He looked at his watch.

Mr Bowling, drugged, looked at his own watch, and filled in that strange pause by standing up.

'You mean,' he said '. . . I am free to go?'

The clock on the mantelpiece ticked, and the Superintendent slowly got to his feet and walked round the large desk to the fireplace.

'Yes,' he said abruptly. 'After I have said this: *it is not easy to hang a man in this country.*' He said, staring at Bowling: 'Do you know that?

'I want you to remember something, Bowling. We have become interested in you. That means a great deal, at Scotland Yard—as many a free but guilty man knows! We are very interested in your previous address, for instance, Number Forty . . . what was it, for the moment it slips me. Thwaite is most interested in you, do you know that, and do you know that we three may one day meet again? Any day. Tomorrow. The day after. Next year.

'The long arm of the law! And then, you were once in an insurance house, you had many clients . . . It was about the time your wife had been killed, that you knew a man called Mr Watson, of Fulham.'

The shadows were falling once again, deepening the corners of the large room. London careered by outside, heading, whether you thought about it or not, towards the end of the war, and towards the appalling problems of peace. Mr Bowling felt as he had felt when a boy, and the master had reminded him coldly that he was a gentleman, and had better never forget it, and had even said he was never to behave like a butcher boy, thus destroying the notion that England was ever a nation of shop-keepers, it was not possible to make friends with those who ran shops—how much harder, then, to work for them? Where did the impoverished gentry find their friends, then? The Superintendent mentioned, coldly, the name of Mr Bowling's old school: it seemed to Mr Bowling the hardest blow of all . . . he had been plucked out of that school, and its much-lauded advantages, and thrown into—what? Into the world at its rawest, and its most changing, a world which had less room for a gentleman than ever unless he had money and powerful relations; and it did seem to Mr Bowling that this was hard. He didn't feel like thinking: 'But character must rise above all this, and talent! A gentleman doesn't murder, does he—he simply goes on the parish, if he has any sense of decency?' He stood rather bent. He had a wish to be in a chapel, playing the organ alone. The sea would be tumbling about outside and the seagulls would be crying. He'd be walking along the ripples on the sand, with Miss Mason, who would have home-made cake ready for their tea. 'This is nice,' he'd say, like a child. 'London, and war, are both far away!' He wouldn't yet say: 'Very soon I must do some war work again.'

'There will never be war,' she might say, 'when people stop forever *forcing* things! We aren't *meant* to achieve very much in this world! Playing the organ well is quite enough?'

'Yes,' he'd say, pleased.

. . . It came to him that the Superintendent was still addressing him, standing before the fire like a human Jehovah, and pointing a great arm at him across the room. The words, quiet and cold, lashed his shoulders, and burned into him. He felt an old and broken man, and the pain of the man writhing and screaming at the triangle could not have been greater. It was an aching, stinging sickness.

There was a pause. Mr Bowling's hands had gone clammy. There seemed to be nothing he could say. How could he explain? He kept his eyes down; it would hardly be cricket to show his sincerity now. Better to remain what he must appear— one more miserable but lucky man they couldn't catch.

Lucky?

He turned and stumbled out of the room and down the stairs, out into the street, and into the welcome dusk.

Lucky?

He walked and walked, in his agony. As he walked he saw himself sinner and saint, finding them strangely the same; and he saw himself on his knees by the cold river water, not the Ganges, but the Thames; and as he bathed his hands, the water reddened; but his hands turned white. He thought only: 'She's saved me. But she won't be there waiting for me, how can she be?' He dared not go to see her.

CHAPTER XXII

BUT he knew he would go to see if he could rest just once again in her now empty room.

He would open the door and go in.

Exhausted and cold, he stumbled and plodded along in the dark, eyes haunted, and tortured mind thinking and singing. To make the punishment fit the crime—the punishment fit the crime!

For what could be greater punishment, than his abject loneliness now?

And supposing the miracle of finding her loyal even now, what greater punishment for him than knowing that any day and any hour, the clutching hand of the law might stretch outward to seize him from her arms and cry:

'Your time is Here and Now—come in.'

Yet, how he prayed for that, for that very thing; that they should have their happiness together, for just a little time: to know what love was, after all the struggle.

He was so sure it was not for him, even to have that. And when he came to her door, and there was no one in the porch or in the hall, there was a silence there which seemed to tell him the truth which frightened him. The nightlight was burning in the hall as before, by the wreath of flowers there.

In the yellow light, he saw that the door of her room was open a little, and it seemed to speak to him for itself.

'She's gone, you poor mutt,' it said. 'Take your time!'

His huge and guilty hand went slowly out to the door, and he saw the ravaged picture of himself, standing there, pleading to the gloom, as he slowly pushed it open.

And yet she was there, in her chair as before, sewing. Now, as strongly as he had known she could not be there, he knew that she would be, waiting for just this moment in all time; the parcel gone, and his guilt gone with it: but herself still there, looking rather shy and awkward, and saying in her unmusical but very kind voice:

'Good evening, Mr Bowling?' And then saying nothing.

It was really too much for a man, thought Mr Bowling. He felt unutterably ashamed, but quite incapable of control; and he sank at once on to his knees by the fire beside her, not facing her, but close to her, and started to cry. It was a dreadful and distressing sound, and even his two great guilty hands couldn't stop it. His shoulders heaved and he felt broken with a new and alarming happiness.

And all she did was to go on sewing for a bit, looking rather embarrassed when he tried to get out between sobs: 'I'm so . . . frightfully sorry, Miss Mason!'

After that she put her knitting down and said: 'Oh, Mr Bowling,' in the kindest voice, and shyly put her arms about him. It was a thing she had not done to a man before, and it only made his sobs sound more dreadful and broken.

She tried very hard to make him stop, but the moment stayed for them both, both always calling each other Miss Mason and Mr Bowling, and both sounding very kind and fond of each other.

And there in the firelight they stayed for a long time, she rocking his large body gently and rather awkwardly to and fro, and saying in her kindly voice:

'Oh, Mr Bowling, don't cry any more! We can go and have walks by the sea! And we can have talks with father! I'm quite sure everything is going to come right?' She rocked him to and fro, and tried to pull his hands from his face. She never once mentioned murder—there was breeding for you! She simply pleaded: 'You really mustn't cry, it makes me so unhappy! There, there,' she said. 'There, there . . . !'

THE END

THE DETECTIVE STORY CLUB

FOR DETECTIVE CONNOISSEURS

recommends

"The Man with the Gun."

Philip MacDonald

Author of Rynox, etc.

MURDER GONE MAD

MR. MacDonald, who has shown himself in *The Noose* and *The Rasp* to be a master of the crime novel of pure detection, has here told a story of a motiveless crime, or at least a crime prompted only by blood lust. The sure, clear thinking of the individual detective is useless and only wide, cleverly organised investigation can hope to succeed.

A long knife with a brilliant but perverted brain directing it is terrorising Holmdale; innocent people are being done to death under the very eyes of the law. Inspector Pyke of Scotland Yard, whom MacDonald readers will remember in previous cases, is put on the track of the butcher. He has nothing to go on but the evidence of the bodies themselves and the butcher's own bravado. After every murder a businesslike letter arrives announcing that another "removal has been carried out." But Pyke "gets there" with a certainty the very slowness of which will give the reader many breathless moments. In the novelty of its treatment, the humour of its dialogue, and the truth of its characterisation, *Murder Gone Mad* is equal to the best Mr. MacDonald has written.

LOOK FOR THE MAN WITH THE GUN

THE DETECTIVE STORY CLUB

FOR DETECTIVE CONNOISSEURS

recommends

"The Man with the Gun."

The Murder of Roger Ackroyd
By AGATHA CHRISTIE

*T*HE MURDER OF ROGER ACKROYD is one of Mrs. Christie's most brilliant detective novels. As a play, under the title of *Alibi*, it enjoyed a long and successful run with Charles Laughton as the popular detective, Hercule Poirot. The novel has now been filmed, and its clever plot, skilful characterisation, and sparkling dialogue will make every one who sees the film want to read the book. M. Poirot, the hero of many brilliant pieces of detective deduction, comes out of his temporary retirement like a giant refreshed, to undertake the investigation of a peculiarly brutal and mysterious murder. Geniuses like Sherlock Holmes often find a use for faithful mediocrities like Dr. Watson, and by a coincidence it is the local doctor who follows Poirot round and himself tells the story. Furthermore, what seldom happens in these cases, he is instrumental in giving Poirot one of the most valuable clues to the mystery.

LOOK FOR THE MAN WITH THE GUN